I Am 我16岁

赵晶颖 ◆ 著

中国青年出版社

(京)新登字 083 号

图书在版编目(CIP)数据

我 16 岁/赵晶颖著. —北京:中国青年出版社,2010.4
ISBN 978-7-5006-9254-6

Ⅰ.①我... Ⅱ.①赵... Ⅲ.①随笔－作品集－中国－当代 Ⅳ.①I267.1

中国版本图书馆 CIP 数据核字(2010)第 053391 号

责任编辑:王飞宁
封面设计:赵晶颖

*

中国青年出版社 出版 发行
社址:北京东四 12 条 21 号 邮政编码:100708
网址:www.cyp.com.cn
编辑部电话:(010)64010551 门市部电话:(010)84039659
保定市新华印刷厂印刷 新华书店经销

*

880×1230 1/32 5.375 印张 2 插页 60 千字
2010 年 4 月北京第 1 版 2010 年 4 月河北第 1 次印刷
定价:15.00 元
本图书如有印装质量问题,请凭购书发票与质检部联系调换
联系电话:(010)84047104

目录

序一　多栖女孩（代序）　_001

序三　_006

作者前言　_013

第一部分：记忆

生活在日本的童年　_003

在加拿大安大略省伦敦市的日子　_011

我们家的小时工——小范阿姨　_019

在北京芳草地小学学习汉语的经历　_025

我心中的文学长官——文佩德　_033

2008年德威Pop Idol　_043

第二部分：文化体验

北京城的奥运之旅　_055

加拿大魁北克市游记　_065

美国游记　_071

西安碑林游记　_079

山西常家大院游记　_085

西班牙游记　_092

第三部分：思考和感悟

老人 _107

海的布鲁斯旋律 _112

历史 _117

黄色的大鸟 _124

Restavek 女孩儿 _134

多元文化与我 _140

后记　十六岁的花季 _149

CONTENTS

Preface II _004

Author's Preface _009

Section One: Memories

My Early Childhood Years—Japan _006

Nostalgia—My Days In London, Canada _014

My Ayi—Xiao Fan _021

Learning Chinese At Beijing Fang Cao Di Elementary School _028

My Captain of Literature—Peder Vinge _037

Dulwich Pop Idol of 2008 _047

Section Two: Cultural Trips

The 2008 Beijing Olympics _058

Quebec City, Canada _067

The United States _074

The Stele Forest, Xi'an _081

The Chang Family courtyard, Shanxi Province _087

Spain _096

Section Three: Thoughts and Inspirations

The Elderly _109

Ocean Blues _114

History _120

The Yellow Bird _129

Restavek Girl _137

Multiculturalism and I _144

序一
多栖女孩（代序）
严歌苓

一个16岁的女孩居住过3个国家，可用3种语言说话，可用两种语言写作，不能不让我想到自己常常调侃自己的"吉卜赛命"。读赵晶颖用两种语言写作的散文和诗歌，我觉得她就是我的年轻版。那种敏感、挣扎以至最终的满足、欢乐，让我温习了自己在30岁后离开本土后的再生以及成长。

我在一篇为自己小说写的序言里，提到一种迁移带来的奇特敏感。从一片热土上拔出自己的根，在一片陌生的土地上一时难以下扎的感觉，陌生的土地再友善，也具有原始的排他性。因此这些裸露的根须如同裸露的神经，对于外界的冷暖，自然是惊人的敏感。杜甫在异乡避兵燹，写出"感时花溅泪"的诗句。李清照客居，也是"才下眉头，又上心头"。李后主当然更是好例子，被掳到敌国，因此"剪不断，理还乱，是离愁"。赵晶颖小小年纪，也多次体味了这类离愁，不敏感也不由得她呀。

那敏感带来活力，也带来疼痛，常常使你不适，积累起来却是成就感和满足感。

赵晶颖的文章和诗,处处让我感觉到这种敏感。她的诗歌《Multiculturalism and I》是她对这种敏感的自白:

I speak,

not knowing what is my mother tongue,

as I have forgotten the language of my birthplace.

I stand,

not knowing where I belong,

as my heritage and nationality differ evidently.

I walk,

not knowing where I will finally settle down,

as I continue to decide among the different lands I have set foot on and cultures I have briefly learnt.

...

All allow me to comprehend:

my roots are not deeply sunk down into the ground,

or fully taking up and assimilating the nutrients

of a particular piece of land.

...

小姑娘请我为她作序,但我认为,没有比这首诗更好的自序了。因为它是赵晶颖16岁人生的缩写,是她文学的、哲学的自画像,是她肉体生命和精神生命最忠实的写照。并且,除了这首诗,她的其他作品都完全是积极的,童心烂漫的。这首诗透露了她在各块国土,以及各种语言、文化、情感方式之间的挣扎、无奈以及些许的疼痛,尽管她在表现疼痛时是勇敢和正面的。

赵晶颖是个幸运的孩子。假如一个没有经历过她所经历的迁移创伤的孩子——生命从熟悉环境往陌生环境的迁移都是创伤性的,在此试着推演弗洛伊德理论:从母亲腹内被出生是人生第一大创伤。因为子宫尽管捆绑你,但熟悉这种捆绑,并把它和安全感化为同样意义,而出生虽然意味着自由,但你要面对一个无边际的陌生世界,所以你立刻把它作为危险来面临。她(他)的情感光谱也许不会像赵晶颖这样七彩齐全。敏感使人情感丰富,这是常识。敏感也导致文学写作,这也是常识。但不是每个人都能获益于这种敏感,甚至不是每一颗心灵都能从这敏感中健全幸存。赵晶颖不仅在这份敏感中苦中作乐,并且大大获益。

谨以我这篇不称职的序言,预祝我的小朋友赵晶颖在文学天空里奋翅起飞,冲上九霄,去见识天外之天。

Preface II

Anyone who knows Amy will not be surprised to note the interest, attention to detail and passion evident in the observations contained in this volume of essays and poems. Independent, astute and reflective, she writes about a broad range of subjects, her fascination in all things revealing a quick mind articulated with sophistication and precision.

The variety of subject matter and depth of concern would be impressive in any collection of prose or poetry, but the fact that Amy is still a student makes these pieces all the more remarkable. We read about her curiosity to understand more about numerous aspects of the world around her: the people who care for and teach her such as her ayi, her English teacher and the motherly shop owner she recalls in London, Ontario. Reading her memories, we feel keenly the sensitivity of a young girl in Japan, seen now through the eyes of maturity. Her lively descriptions of Xi'an, Madrid and California vividly evoke not only the locations she depicts but also the wonder and reflection of a thoughtful young woman.

That Amy is a talented artist and photographer will be obvious to the reader in the perceptive analysis of her experiences and most particularly in the imagery of her poems. She surprises us with her ambitious choice of subject matter, provoking reflection and demanding strong responses with her impassioned deliberations on history and multiculturalism. Additionally, a musical quality pervades her verse, her sensitivity to language further exemplifying her ardent nature, and the convincing drama of her empathetic poem, 'Yellow Bird Scene' assures us of her capacity to imagine, feel and understand.

Not only will the essays and poems in this volume provide the reader with entertainment and thought-provoking insights, they will provoke sometimes-uncomfortable reflections on the parts we all play in our world.

Rosie Edwards

Beijing, October 2009

序三

赵晶颖同学是一位令每一位作为她的老师的人都会感到骄傲的学生,无论她的品格,还是在学业上显示的才华。作为她的中文老师,从过往连同未来总共不过4年的时间,但我从她以及她身后的这样一个群体的身影的晃动中,总是思考:这是怎样的一代人?他们今后将怎样影响这个世界?自己能为孩子的现在、未来做些什么?晶颖同学的这本书,某种意义上是在提示我们老师、家长和成人世界的每一员,对于一个在国际环境、多元文化背景下长大的孩子,他们经历着怎样的心路历程:人类丰富的文化遗产有多少令他们孜孜吮吸,有多少又带给他们压力与困惑?

全书共分为3部分:散文、游记、诗歌。它标志着一个孩童成长的过程,也预示了其未来成长的方向:由自我走向他者。

散文部分:关注自己生活中的喜怒哀愁,记录身边出现的那些人物的良善与美德——尽管他们肤色各异,文化多元,他们共同构建了"我"童年的经验,建立了"我"最初的价值观,涂抹出"我"未来的精神底色。

游记部分：这已成为国际学校的学生很重要的生活、学习方式。他们不仅在课本中学，不仅通过网络等高科技的传媒获取知识，他们依然愿意回归原始的学习方式——徒步行走。他们要调动各种感官去深刻触摸产生这丰沃的知识文化的每一寸土地、每一棵草木，去访问探查这土地上滋养的每一个生命。

诗歌部分：这正是前两种的积累对未来的指向——影响与改变世界。由于这种特殊的学习环境以及接触的人群，整个世界的政治、经济变化似乎就发生在我们身边，同学的来来往往就是一幅国际关系的晴雨表，我们的友谊不允许我们无视，我们的困惑也正由此开始……

美国的著名宗教领袖马丁·路德金在德克斯特教会的布道中，曾有过一段对"完整生命的三个层面"的表述，即任何完整的生命都包括这三个层面：长、宽和高。生命的长度并不是他的延续与寿数，而是生命要达至他的个人目标与理想的向前动力，那是人对自身福祉的内向关怀；生命的宽度是对他人福利的外向关怀；生命的高度则是一个人向上的对神的追求。

晶颖同学以及这一群体的同学们可能较其他同龄人更早地开启"完整生命"的建造，因为时代在他们身上注入了特殊的使命，我们也不敢懈怠——

翻开扉页，步入一个游学东西、用双语讲述自己的故事的年轻心灵,探索一条道路,那是我们所未曾经历过的。

周岩(汉语老师)

2009年9月28日凌晨,草于北苑

Author's Preface

Whenever people ask me—where are you from? I always hesitate. Although it seems like a simple question, its answer is a fundamental part of a person's identity. As a girl with a Chinese heritage who was born in Japan, grew up in Canada and started living in Beijing at the age of eight, I have always mused on how to answer it pertinently. Now, unwilling to exclude any part of my being, I always reply: "I am a Chinese Canadian born in Japan." The response to my answer is always along the lines of "that's complicated"—which is true; I have been embraced by a multicultural environment for the past sixteen years.

While experiencing constant changes to the languages I was exposed to, I began to develop a keen interest in the culture of different languages, and became familiar with its charm. I have come to acknowledge how the various aspects of communication such as grammar, tone, emphasis, accents and rhythm in language, can reflect the different traits and customs of each culture. My experience of speaking Japanese, English and Mandarin, as well as acquiring a few years of French and Spanish in between, have nurtured my desire to explore all languages. This is the reason why, with paltry Chinese skills, I had the courage to enroll in a local Chinese elementary school, and earned the 1st prize in a Chinese competition among international middle school students two years later. At the same time, it formed the basis of my decision to write this bilingual book.

As I traversed the globe, becoming acquainted with diverse cultures and communicating with people of different ethnic backgrounds, I became cognizant of the fact that there is a growing population of Third-Culture Kids (Global Nomads) with similar experiences to mine in the world right now. The rapid development of international schools in Beijing serves to corroborate this fact. We are associated with and responsible for affairs of the future economy, politics and cultural exchange of the global society to a considerable extent. As a member of this group, I wish to exploit my bilingual ability to record my stories of growing up and, as a result, reflect the knowledge, perspectives and thoughts of Third-Culture Kids. Every piece of writing in this book recalls a segment of the multicultural journey that I have traveled over the past sixteen years. I sincerely hope that this volume can serve as a medium through which I can share my experiences and truthful emotions with the young individuals of my generation.

This book is assembled as a collection of essays, travel writing and poems in both English and Mandarin. The difference in these two languages alone has allowed me to further discover and acknowledge the similarities and differences between the Western and Chinese cultures. Before you flip through these pages, I wish to beg your indulgence for the flaws in this publication, as this is my first foray into writing as well as translating a book. Also, I have highlighted and defined certain English words which I consider to be more difficult or specialized than others in Mandarin. I hope this selection of vocabulary will aid Chinese readers and contribute to the development of their interest in the English language. I also hope that the Chinese section of the book can assist international English readers with their learning of Chinese.

  Finally, I would like to thank Ms. Yan GeLing, who kindly offered time to write a proem for my petty book. I would like to express my gratitude towards my former English teacher, Ms. Rosie Edwards, and my Chinese teacher, Ms. Zhou Yan for taking so much of their time and effort to proofread my work and also write prefaces for my book. I would also like to give many thanks to my former Chinese teacher from Beijing World Youth Academy, Ms. He JiPing for her considerations and support, and also for the short commentary that she generously agreed to write for this book. Last but not least, this book would not be possible without the ceaseless support and encouragement from my loving family: Mum, Dad and my Grandparents; it would also have been impossible without my friends, who have shared some of the most valuable experiences in life with me, which make an indispensable part of the content of this book. I thank you all with greatest sincerity.

Amy Zhao

Beijing, Autumn 2009

作者前言

当人们问我"你是哪里人?"这个简单的问题时,我总会犹豫一下。这个问题虽然简单,但它却询问了一个人最基本的背景。作为一个祖籍是中国、出生在日本、童年生长在加拿大、8岁来到北京生活的女孩,我时常考虑如何能更贴切地回答它。因为不想遗漏上述的任何一点,我的回答常常是:"我是一个出生在日本的加籍华人。"对方的反应通常是:"这么复杂啊!"而这个回应更让我意识到我的成长背景的确不那么简单,因为至今为止的16年,我始终生活在多元文化的环境里。

在我的成长经历中,随着不断变迁的语言环境,我对语言文化的兴趣也越来越浓厚,觉得语言有着它神奇的魅力。通过不同的语言表述,能反映出不同文化的特征和美学。从日语到英语再到汉语,中途还夹学了一段时间法语和西班牙语,使我对语言的好奇、学习和探索的欲望也越发强烈。特别当我8岁来到中国后,在汉语方面可以说是一窍不通的状况下,为了掌握它,我带着勇气进入了当地的小学,从五年级上到毕业。就是在这两年中，我的汉语水平有了很大提高。这段经历促成我后来在国际学生初中汉语作文比赛中拿到了一等奖，并且在北京举办的国际学校汉语比赛中取得了第一名。这一切都为我用双语写作奠定了基础。

在计划写作的思考过程中，我意识到：和我有着类似经历的同龄人、同代人有很多。仅从北京国际学校的建立和迅速发展中就足以证明这一点。在多元文化熏陶下成长的我们已经形成了一个庞大的群体。随着这个群体的成长和壮大，可以预测未来的我们将与世界政治、经济和文化发展的互动更为紧密、显著和频繁。同时，这个群体在国际社会所起的作用和担负的责任也会更加突出。因此，作为这个群体中一员的我，希望通过语言文字的记述，把有着一定代表性的这个群体的成长足迹、思维模式和喜怒哀乐记载下来。这无疑是个非常有意义的过程。

这本书的写作，对于我来说，是一段很有价值且受益匪浅的经历。通过一段段文字，一篇篇文章，系统地追忆、回顾和感悟了这16年来在多元文化旅程中的自我成长历程，同时也对自我有了更深的认识，对多元文化的实质和影响力也有了更全面的理解和评估。我希望通过一个16岁的中学生的多元文化经历，使每一位生活和学习背景异同的读者能与我在不同程度上思考和感受多元文化对我们这一代青年人的渗透和影响，同时与我分享在多元文化的旅程中所留下的真切体验和不同视角。

本书用中英文两种语言书写，以作文、游记和诗歌的文体形式回忆、记述了一些16年来在多元文化背景下我的成长体验、情感和感悟。在用中英文写作的过程中，两种语言的不同之处促使我在文字运用的基础上，更进一步探索和学习了中西文化的异同。读此书之前，敬请读者们对文章互译的不足之处给予谅解。特别是本书的第三部分——诗歌，因为在结构上、语言的个性化程度和细腻的情感表达方面，相对来说难度更大一些。

在本书的英文部分，我对一些自认为有一定难度或是专业性较强的词汇做了简明的中文注释。希望这些注解可以帮助以中文为主要阅读语言的读者们在阅读过程中增添对英语学习的兴趣。同时，也期望中文部分可以给西方或以英文为主要阅读语言的朋友们在接触和学习汉语方面尽一份绵薄之力。

最后，我要感谢著名文学家、作家严歌苓在百忙之中为此书作序。感谢我在德威的现任中文老师周岩，和前任英文老师Rosie Edwards，在百忙之中给我的文稿提出宝贵的建议和修改意见，并感谢她们为此书撰写的导言。感谢我的前校世青中学的中文老师何济平对我的关心、支持和为本书所作的阅读感言。也要感谢我的家人对我写作的肯定和鼓励。我还要感谢我的新老朋友们，因为若没有他们给我带来的不同内心感受及多彩的记忆,就没有此书的写作基础。再次真诚地谢谢大家。

赵晶颖

2009年深秋

I.
MEMORIES...
记忆

1998 AUTUMN, IN CANADA
一九九八年 秋，加拿大

生活在日本的童年

(高一)

我出生在日本,4岁以前一直生活在那里,能讲一口流利的日语。因为年龄太小,那时的生活在我的记忆里只留下了一些片段。但即使只存有片段的记忆,当我提笔回忆时,我的心里依然感觉很亲切、温暖和快乐。

记得每年三四月,是樱花盛开的时节,父母总会带着我去赏花。樱花的具体模样我已记不清了,只记得小小的我穿着一件粉色带白领子的裙子,指着那一片片透明的粉白色盛开的樱花惊奇地对妈妈说:"妈妈,看!粉色的玻璃!"现在想起来,那种感觉还犹如梦幻。在樱花树下的我不停地跑来跑去,因为赏花的人太多了,爸爸总会紧跟在我后面,怕我走失。大人们赏花时,我就会去找食摊上的各种小吃。我最喜欢吃的就是那个与樱花颜色差不多的年糕球串(dango)。当樱花瓣洒落满地的时候,各种各样的花相继绽放,美丽的春天又来了!

春去夏来,每年8月份的夏季节日(Matsuri)是我最快乐的日子。印象很深的就是平时穿着工作服忙碌的男男女女们都穿上了传统的夏季和服(yukata)。记得那时妈妈给我穿的是一件白色带五颜六色印花的yukata,腰上系一条粉红色的丝带,脚上穿着夹脚的小木屐,走起路来还"咔哒咔哒"地响。到了傍晚,街道上的人越来越多,人们穿着漂亮的传统和服,吃着香喷喷的传统日餐,哼唱着传统的日本演歌,路边还摆着各种各样供孩子们玩耍的设施,特别热闹,就像一个小小的游乐园。街道被各式各样用特殊的纸做成的彩灯照亮着,大人们喝酒聊天,孩子们在一旁玩耍嬉闹,我总是会玩到筋疲力尽。但至今让我记忆犹新的是Matsuri结束的第二天清晨,妈妈送我上保育院的路上,经过前一天还摆满五颜六色的小摊,热闹非凡的街道时,发现一切都消失了,安静了,恢复了以前的样子。我不解地问妈妈:"怎么都没了?到哪儿去了?"妈妈说:"都收拾干净了呀。"我心里很纳闷儿地想:天啊,这难道是魔术吗?这么快就都没了吗?真的就没了吗?我边走边回头,两个眼睛不停地从上转到下,从左转到右,很不情愿地证实:没了,真的没了⋯⋯

秋去冬来,记得那是我初进幼儿园的第一个冬天。我和其他入园的新生都换上了黑绿格的园服:女孩子们穿裙裤,男孩子们穿短裤,再配一顶黑色小礼帽,看起来很可爱,我特别喜欢。但让我吃惊的是,即便在严冬,我们也只穿膝盖以下的白色棉袜,真的很冷,可老师们每天早上都会把我们带出去跑步。记得有的小朋友因为怕冷,不愿意出来,但最后还是被老师领了出来。大家在寒冷中跑着、跳着、做着游戏,慢慢就感觉身体暖和了起来。那时妈妈可心疼我了,一回家就给我换上厚厚的连裤长袜。开始因为怕冷所以我很期待暖和的长袜,但后来我习惯了,就常把妈妈刚给我穿上的长袜脱下来。我不但没感冒,体质反而越来越壮了。那时的我,就像一个健壮的小武士。现在妈妈也常说,我性格中的一种坚持和毅力或许是从那时培养出来的。

  1997年的初秋,我随父母离开日本迁居加拿大,虽然一直还没有机会回去过,但在那里度过的童年的喜乐却时常会浮现在我脑海中。

My Early Childhood Years—Japan

(Grade 10)

Until the age of four, I lived in Japan and spoke in fluent Japanese. Because I was still very young when I lived in Japan, I can only remember bits and pieces of my life at that time, but even so, when I pick up my pen to write about these memories I have carefully gathered, I still feel an indescribable[①] sense of familiarity, warmth and happiness.

I remember that every year, cherry blossoms[②] would bloom in the month of March or April, and my parents would take me to see the flowers. I only vaguely[③] remember what the cherry blossoms looked like, but I do recall myself standing below the flower trees, wearing a white-collared pink dress, pointing at the huge, translucent[④] patch of pinkish-white blossoms as I said to my mother: "Mom, look! It's pink glass!" The place simply made me feel like I was inside a dream. I remember I always ran between the cherry blossom trees in excitement, and my father would chase behind me to keep me within his sight, worried that I would get lost in the crowd. When the adults were still flower-viewing, I would search for various treats sold at the food stalls[⑤]. My favorite was sticky rice ball skewers[6] (dango), which came in the same colors—pink and white—as the cherry blossoms. Cherry blossoms were spring's messengers; as their petals began to fall and slowly cover the ground, other flowers would start to bloom subsequently[7], heralding[8] the arrival of another spring...

As summer gradually arrived, replacing spring, it was a sign that the annual[9] Matsuri (summer festival) would soon arrive in the month of August. When the festival began, people would change from their usual work clothes into the traditional yukata (summer kimono). I remember I would wear a white yukata with colorful flower prints on it with a long pinkish-red ribbon tied around my waist and the traditional wooden flip-flops[10] that made a "clank-clank" sound when I walked around. At dawn, the streets would be their busiest. Everyone wore traditional clothes, ate traditional food and some hummed traditional Japanese folk songs. The streets were lit up by lanterns[11] of different colors, shapes and sizes and adults chatted[12] amongst themselves as children played games at different stalls. The atmosphere was like that of a miniature[13] amusement park.

¶I remember when my mother and I passed the same streets the next morning, I was utterly[14] shocked by what I saw: everything was gone; the streets looked exactly how they had before the festival. I asked my mother in great disbelief: "How did it all disappear?" My mother said: "They cleaned everything up overnight." I thought to myself: Wow, that's really fast. Had it anything to do with magic? Is it possible that everything could have disappeared so fast? Is it really all gone?... As I walked down the streets, I kept turning back and looked around in all directions, and finally, to my disappointment, came to conclude that everything was gone, truly gone…

When autumn passed, winter's chilly wind blew the wilted leaves away, leaving the trees bare. I still clearly remember my first winter at my nursery school, when we all changed into our winter uniform: girls wore black and green plaid skorts, boys wore shorts of the same pattern, and we all had a black, stiff[15]-brimmed[16] hat which I loved to wear. What surprised me the most was that even in such cold weather, we were still only allowed to wear socks that were below knee-length. In the beginning I was freezing, but our teacher would take our whole class to run around the small schoolyard every morning. Some students, scared of the cold, did not want to go outside at first, but were eventually brought out by our teacher. Once everyone was outside, we were urged to run and participate in every game in order to keep ourselves warm in the cold. When I got home, my mother would always make me change into longer socks, but as I slowly became more immune[17] to the cold from running outside everyday, I began to refuse to wear them. Because of this, my mother became very worried, as she thought I might get sick. But she gradually realized that the exercise had strengthened my constitution[18], and thus I rarely caught a cold. Looking back, as a child,

I was like an indefatigable⑲ little soldier. My mother sometimes says that the toughness and persistence⑳ in my character probably developed from this childhood experience…

In the beginning of the autumn in 1997, I left Japan and moved to Canada with my parents. Ever since then, I have never had the opportunity to go back and visit, but pieces of memory of my childhood in Japan still often come to mind, and leave a smile on my face whenever they do…

---

1 indescribable adj. 难以形容的: They have experienced indescribable hardship.

2 Cherry blossoms n.(复数) 樱花:Many tourists took pictures under the cherry blossom trees.

3 Vaguely adv. 模糊地:I can only vaguely remember what my great grandmother looked like.

4 Translucent adj. 半透明的:The windows are made of translucent glass.

5 Stalls n. (复数)铺子,摊子:There were long queues at the stalls.

6 Skewers n.(复数)串:She loves to eat chicken skewers.

7 Subsequently adv. 随后，相继:After the discovery, further investigations were carried out subsequently.

8 Heralding v. (进行时)宣布或预报将要发生的事: The people's huge discontentment herald [ed] (过去时)a rebellion.

9 Annual adj. 每年的:The Quebec Winter Carnival is a famous annual event that takes place in Quebec, Canada.

10 Flip-flops n. 夹脚拖鞋:We all wore our flip-flops to the beach.

11 Lanterns n. 灯笼:During the Chinese New Year, many people would buy red lanterns to decorate their doors.

12 Chatted v. (过去时)谈天:A group of women chatted inside the café.

13 Miniature adj. 小型的:The model displayed miniature

versions of each building in the compound.

14 Utterly adj. 极为;完全:She was utterly shocked when Jim told her about the news.

15 Stiff adj. 坚硬的:The stiff collars of his shirt made him feel uncomfortable.

16 Brimmed adj. 带边的:She always wears her brimmed hat when it is sunny.

17 Immune adj. 对……免疫:He seems to be immune to criticism.

18 Constitution n. 体格,体质:Although her diet plan helped her lose weight, it weakened her constitution.

19 Indefatigable adj. 不会感到劳累的;充满活力的: He has an indefatigable work ethic.

20 Persistence n. 坚持,毅力:Persistence is one of the main keys to success.

在加拿大安大略省伦敦市的日子

(初三)

一晃7年过去了,我已度过了7个没有加拿大的枫叶陪伴的秋天。虽然7年的时间并不短,但7年前的那段日子却依然记忆犹新。

儿时的我最爱加拿大的秋天,每当秋天来临,几乎每天,我都会趴在窗口望着一片片树叶渐渐地换下绿装,变成一个个衣着华丽的"贵妇",色彩缤纷。每天上下学的路上,我都会和母亲走在宽宽的人行道上,边说边笑,或者唱着学校新学的歌。我们同一片片在秋风中旋转起舞的枫叶一起跳动着,全心地融入那浪漫的金黄和酒红的秋色中。

加拿大的伦敦是一个鲜为人知的城市,在那里居住的人不多,同住一个小区的人们基本都认识,相互之间都很亲善。我经常在离家不远的小店串门,跟店主聊天,结识了不少友善的人们,其中给我印象最深的是带着一些神秘色彩的巴巴拉夫人。她是一间装饰品店的老板,身材圆润,总是把头发系成一个滚圆的小球。我最喜欢她那永远浮现在脸颊上的让人感到无比温暖的微笑。几乎每天放学,我都会推开那扇发出

"吱呀"响声的小木门,随着一阵悦耳的铃铛声走进她的小店。每次她都会热情地招待我这位小客人,从不怠慢,并给我看她觉得最有趣的装饰品,给我讲述它们背后的故事。在那里,我开始喜欢上了美术,并变得喜好观察和想象,因为巴巴拉夫人的店就如精彩的魔幻世界,使我对货柜上的每一件饰物都充满好奇与虔敬。

除了和善意有趣的人们交往,我还结识了维多利亚公园的小松鼠们。第一次相遇,它们似乎很怕我,一溜烟儿就跑掉了。可在后来两年的时间里,我们渐渐熟了,每次看到我,它们就跳着跑着到我面前,用一种期待和顽皮的眼神向我索要食物。我常常会喂给它们面包或桑果,但若我没带食物,就会到附近的咖啡店买几片胡萝卜面包作为补偿。有一天,我发现它们居然能快速地用那小小的牙啃掉葡萄皮,吐掉葡萄籽儿,吞进葡萄肉,简直太神奇了!至今,小家伙们顽皮的模样和我给它们起的名字我都还记得,有时,它们还会蹦入我的梦中。

离开加拿大伦敦的那一天我永远都不会忘记。当我和父母拖着大行李箱从公寓走出来时,保安皮特送给了我一只很大的奶白色玩具熊作为道别礼物;一对做小生意的韩国双胞胎哥哥从店里给我精心挑选了可爱的贴纸;巴巴拉夫人从那棵还没有来得及收起的圣诞树上取下了我最喜爱的水晶天使饰物,并说:"孩子,无论你在哪里,只要你想起这里,它的魔法就会把你带回来。有机会就回来看看,这里永远都是你的家。"我含着眼泪,抱着巴巴拉夫人说:"我会的!我会回来的!我不会忘记你和这里的一切!"

如今,当我站在窗口凝视着北京城繁华喧闹的街头时,常会想起在加拿大伦敦的那段愉快而宁静的生活。一次,当我拿出水晶天使并紧握它的双翼时,巴巴拉夫人的笑容,保安皮特、双胞胎哥哥们,连同那群上蹿下跳的小松鼠的身影,又在木门的"吱呀"声和那清脆的铃铛声中,拉开了我思乡的帘幕。

"啊!"我情不自禁地叫出声来。真的,就如巴巴拉夫人所说的,水晶天使把我带回了家。

NOSTALGIA—MY DAYS IN LONDON, CANADA

(Grade 9)

Six years have passed in the blink of an eye, and I have experienced six autumns without my favored companion—the Canadian maple leaves. Although six years is surely not a short period of time, the stories that took place in London, Ontario, which have now carefully grown into nagging childhood memories, still project[①] clearly from my mind.

When I was a little girl, I admired Canadian autumns. When autumn swept the hot summer away, I would always lean against my apartment window and anticipate Autumn's touch: the leaves shedding their petite[②] green coats to reveal themselves as gorgeous duchesses in rich colored gowns. Everyday, I would walk to and from school with my mother, hand-in-hand, laughing and singing the new songs I learnt in music class. On those autumn days, I would twirl with the "duchesses" who cared for a quick but mesmerizing[③] dance in the air before they pirouetted to the ground, forming a romantic essence of gold and wine red.

London, Ontario is a city inhabited by few and known

by fewer. The tight-knit community knew each other well and treated one another with familiarity. I used to always hop into shops nearby my apartment for a short conversation with the owners, enjoying many valuable friendships that I still cherish[4].

One friend who first comes to mind is the owner of my favorite antique shop—Mrs. Barbra. She was a plump[5] lady around the age of fifty, who habitually[6] tied her grizzled[7] hair into a little round ball. What I loved most about her was that wrinkled smile she always wore that never failed to warm my heart. Every time I walked past her shop from school, I would push open that familiar creaky wooden door and enter, accompanied by a series of melodious[8] lively bells hanging above the entrance.

Mrs. Barbra never treated her small guest with a lack of hospitality[9]. She would take out various little ornaments[10] and paintings and tell me intriguing[11] stories about each of them. I believe it was around then that I began to love and appreciate art, and became increasingly more observant and imaginative. She made me realize that every object can embody[12] infinite tales and instantly spring into life through a story-telling tongue. Mrs. Barbra's shop was a magical place to me, and that impression made me treat every object on the shelves with the ultimate respect and caution.

Not only did I make friends with many people in the neighborhood, I also had a group of squirrels in Victoria Park as playmates. Our first encounter[13] was a rather hasty one—the squirrels disappeared instantly into the bushes at the first glimpse㉔ of me. But during my two years in London, we came to know each other. They would scamper⑮ towards me every time I visited and stare innocently at me with beady eyes, which I learnt to interpret⑯ as their request for food. Sometimes when I forgot to prepare breadcrumbs or nuts in a Ziploc bag, I would buy two slices of carrot bread from the nearby coffee shop to feed them. During our days together, I made a fascinating discovery: I realized that when they ate grapes, they could use their two tiny front teeth to nibble⑰ off the peel and deftly spit out the seeds at a surprisingly fast speed. I can still recall their naughty expressions and some of the names I gave them. They even bounce their way into my dreams from time to time.

I will never forget the day I left for China. When I came down from my apartment with my parents, clumsily dragging my oversized luggage, Pete the security guard came up to me with a big fluffy beige bear as a goodbye gift. The Korean twin brothers who owned the "Artbox" store a few blocks down the street sent me a selection of stickers to add to my sticker book and Mrs. Barbra took off the crystal angel ornament that I had adored⑱ from the still unremoved Christmas tree as she said softly: "Child, no matter where in the world you are, whenever you are overcome with nostalgia and miss London, this angel will take you back here. Don't forget to come back and visit sometime, here will always be your home." My eyes swam with tears which streamed uncontrollably down my cheeks as I flung myself into Mrs. Barbra's arms for our last hug: "I will miss this place... Oh I will... I will remember you and everything here forever!"

Now, when I stare out at the busy streets of Beijing filled with constant honking and traffic lights, I often miss Canada's tranquil⑲ ambiance⑳. Once, when I squeezed the angel's wings, I saw Mrs. Barbra's warm wrinkled smile; Pete and the Korean twin brothers' familiar faces; and the jumping figures of the squirrels, and faintly heard the creaking of Mrs. Barbra's wooden door, along with the tinkling of bells above it.

I cried out in astonishment㉑. Yes, just as Mrs. Barbra had said, my crystal angel had taken me back home...

---

1 Project v. 突出:A small piece of paper project [ed] (过去时) from the book.

2 Petite adj. (在这里指衣服的大小)超小号:All of the coats in this shop are available in petite sizes.

3 Mesmerizing adj. 使迷惑或眼花缭乱的:The woman's mesmerizing stare attracted all the men in the ballroom.

4 Cherish v. 珍惜:I will always cherish the memories that I have shared with friends who will be leaving next school year.

5 Plump adj. 圆胖的;敦实的:Her plump body resembled that of a ball.

6 Habitually adv. 习惯性地:He habitually bites his nails when he is nervous.

7 Grizzled adj. 花白的:The lady's grizzled hair suggested her old age.

8 Melodious adj. 悦耳的:The birds chirped a melodious tune.

9 Hospitality n. 好客的表现;殷勤地接待客人:Mr. Jackson always treats his guests with great hospitality.

10 Ornaments n. (复数的)装饰物:My family and I went to buy ornaments for our Christmas tree last week.

11 Intriguing adj. 吸引人的:Our appetizer for dinner was an intriguing combination of French and Japanese.

12 Embody v. 包含:The answer to the riddle was embod[ied] (过去分词) in the carvings on the ancient tablet.

13 Encounter n. 意外,简短的相见:After the brief encounter, we both went our separate ways.

14 Glimpse n. 瞥见:The victim only caught a glimpse of his attacker before she was knocked out.

15 Scamper v. 蹦跳:The puppy scamper[ed] (过去式) towards the door as he heard its owner's footsteps.

16 Interpret v. 理解,领会:The meaning of the poem is very difficult to interpret.

17 Nibble v. 啃:The baby nibbled at her food.

18 Adored v. (过去时)非常喜爱:She adores all of the handicrafts sold in this shop.

19 Tranquil adj. 安静的;平静的:The sea was tranquil at night.

20 Ambiance n. 环境;周围:The relaxed ambiance of the café is popular with its customers.

21 Astonishment n. 惊讶:The girl jumped in great astonishment.

我们家的小时工——小范阿姨

(高二)

在我读高一前,当每天早上听到"叮咚叮咚"的门铃时,就是家里的小时工小范阿姨来了。小范阿姨不到30岁,个子不高,有着宽宽的肩膀,有力的双臂和结实的双腿,看起来非常敦实健壮。她圆圆的脸白里透红,像秋天的红苹果洋溢着青春的活力。她有一双不大但却有神的眼睛,鼻子有点扁,扁中带有几分可爱,厚厚的嘴唇总是喜欢哼着带有安徽方言的小调儿:"小妹妹,你坐船头……"但我从来没听她把歌完整地唱下来过。她的声音很特别,音调总是在高八度的区域里,即使用很小的声音说话,也照样会给你的耳膜带来高频的冲击。即便在打电话的时候,也会让人误以为她在跟谁吵架。

别看她个儿小,干起活儿来却十分麻利。只是在干活儿的过程中,你偶尔会听到"啪"或"砰"的声音,不是一个碗被打碎了,就是一个玻璃球被碰裂了,要么就是一只调羹身首两处。之后,她总是呆呆地站在那儿,一动不动地望着地上的碎片,喃喃自语:"不知怎么搞的,突然掉下来了……"看着她那一脸无奈而又略带紧张和歉疚的样子,我哭笑不得,家里人也因此不忍心过多地责怪她,只是提醒她下次注意。

给我记忆最深的是在我上小学五六年级的时候,那时,因妈妈身体不太好,小范阿姨每天早上6点半左右都会来为我准备早餐。不管是严冬酷暑,还是风雨交加;不管是她家中有事,还是途中自行车出故障了,她都会准时赶来,从未耽误过。记得一天清晨,雷电交加,大雨倾盆,听到外面隆隆的雷声和哗哗的雨声,我心想:今天小范阿姨肯定来不了了。正当我准备打开冰箱找点东西吃的时候,忽然听到"叮咚叮咚"那熟悉而又意外的门铃声。开门一看,竟是小范阿姨湿漉漉地站在门口。她整个裤腿都被雨淋湿了,雨披上沾着大泥点,头发也不停地往下滴水。她告诉我说,因为怕迟到,她拼命骑车赶时间,由于地面太滑,摔了一跤。我心里即刻涌出一股暖流,有一种说不出的感动。

我上高一那年,小范阿姨因为要回老家生孩子,不得不决定离开她工作了6年的地方——我的家。她要离开的那几天,我心里酸酸的,有一种深深的不舍。在相处的6年中,她似乎成为了我们家庭中的一员。

没有小范阿姨的日子让我不习惯了很长时间。直到今天,我仍然会常常想起她和她那熟悉的安徽地方小调:"小妹妹,你坐船头……"

My Ayi①—Xiao Fan

(Grade 8)

Before tenth grade, whenever I heard my doorbell ring in the morning, I would expect my ayi, Xiao Fan. Xiao Fan ayi was a little less than thirty years old, fairly short in height but with a stout② figure of broad shoulders and tough arms and legs. She had a round face with flushed③ red cheeks which resembled④ an apple at harvest time and was filled with liveliness and energy. She had small but bright eyes and a flat nose that suggested her affable⑤ character; her thick lips always hummed⑥ the same tune with an An Hui accent: "Xiao mei mei, ni zuo chuan tou..." but I never heard her finish the complete song. Her voice was quite distinctive⑦; her tone was always in high octaves⑧. Even when she spoke softly, you would still feel a considerable impact⑨ on your eardrums. Sometimes when she was on the phone, people would mistakenly believe that she was having an argument with someone.

Although Xiao Fan ayi was not significant in height, she was a swift⑩ worker who always completed her housekeeping tasks in a relatively short amount of time. But during her work, we would sometimes jump to a bang or a shattering sound. When this happened, it would either be a shattered bowl, a cracked glass ball or a halved ceramic⑪ soupspoon, and we would see Xiao Fan ayi staring at the mess, dumbfounded⑫, while muttering to herself: "I don't know how, it just suddenly fell..." Looking at her innocent, helpless and slightly nervous and apologetic⑬ face, my family and I never had the heart to scold her, but only reminded her that she should be more careful.

What I remember the most is when I was still in fifth and sixth grade, due to my mother's ill health, Xiao Fan ayi would always come to my house at six o'clock in the morning to prepare breakfast for me. No matter if the weather was extreme or her bike broke down on the way, she would still find a way to arrive on time and never missed one of my breakfasts. I remember one morning, there was a thunderstorm, and as I heard the deafening⑭ thunder and pouring rain, I felt quite sure that Xiao Fan ayi would not be coming. Right when I was about to prepare my own breakfast, I suddenly heard that familiar but unexpected doorbell. I opened the door and saw Xiao Fan ayi standing there, sopping⑮ wet. The legs of her trousers were completely drenched⑯, her poncho⑰ was muddy and water kept dripping down from her hair. She told me that she had been cycling in a rush, worried that she would be late, and because the ground was too slippery, she had fallen off her bike. I instantly felt a surge of warmth within me and was left with only pure gratitude.

When I began my first year in high school, Xiao Fan

ayi had to go back to her hometown to give birth to her new baby. During the few days before she left, I was very upset and was unwilling to let her go. She had worked in our house for six years, and she seemed to have grown to become part of the family.

It took a long time for me to get used to not having Xiao Fan ayi working in our house, and even now, more than a year after she left, I still miss her. Whenever I think of her, that same An Hui tune plays inside my head: "Xiao mei mei, ni zuo chuan tou..."

---

1 Ayi n. (英语拼音)指中文的"阿姨": My family hired a new ayi from Si Chuan.

2 Stout adj. 强壮的: The middle-aged man had a stout figure.

3 Flushed adj. 通红的(脸蛋): The mother was worried about her baby's flushed and hot cheeks.

4 Resembled v. (过去时)与什么相似: When Jane was a child, her looks closely resembled that of her sister's.

5 Affable adj. 友善的, 平易近人的: Susie's affable character is loved by everyone.

6 Hummed v. (过去时)哼: The mother quietly hummed a lullaby to put her baby to sleep.

7 Distinctive adj. 与众不同的, 特殊的: She has a distinctive fashion style that catches many people's attention.

8 Octaves n. (复数)八音度: The African-American female singer can impressively reach up to four octaves.

9 Impact n. 冲击, 影响: The bright colors used in the painting gave an immense visual impact.

10 Swift adj. 迅速的, 熟练的: My aunt carried the stack of plates to the kitchen in a swift manner.

11 Ceramic adj. 陶瓷的: I took my foreign friend to a local market to buy ceramic cups and plates as gifts for her

parents.

12 (Be) Dumbfounded v. (过去分词)惊呆:The audience was completely dumbfounded when Katie sang her first note.

13 Apologetic adj. 抱歉的:The waitress was very apologetic about spilling water on the customer's shirt.

14 Deafening adj. 震耳欲聋的:The loudspeakers blasted out deafening heavy metal music.

15 Sopping adj. 浑身湿透的:She hung her sopping clothes on the drying rack.

16 (Be) Drenched adj. (过去分词)湿透的:By the time Sammie reached home, she was completely drenched from walking in the rain.

17 Poncho n. 雨披:She forgot her poncho at home, so she had to buy one from the supermarket.

在北京芳草地小学学习汉语的经历

(初一)

在蒙特梭利国际小学读到四年级毕业,父母决定送我去本地芳草地小学的国际部就读小学五、六年级,目的是提高我的汉语水平,这对于从小一直在国际学校上学的我无疑是一个很大的挑战。四年级的暑假,妈妈把芳草地的汉语和数学课本都复印了一遍,希望我每天用相当一部分时间来预习。但由于在数学方面,国际学校与本地学校内容、进度上相差比较大,我只好把大部分精力都放在了数学上,汉语的补修也就自然没有太多时间了。

入学考试那天,数学和英语都顺利考完,自我感觉也不错。在最后的汉语考试时,老师先发给我四年级水平的汉语试卷,一看试卷,绝大部分试题都不会,我蒙了,差一点儿哭出来。监考老师发现了这一点,走过来问我要不要试试三年级水平的试卷。我木然地点点头,但突然感觉一阵紧张,生怕下一张卷子我也不会做。拿到卷子后,我略微松了口气,虽然有不少不会的题,但还是有一些我能回答的。于是我尽量让自己冷静下来,努力把所知道的答案写出来,可卷子还没做完,时间就到了。我匆忙写上自己的名字,把卷子交了上去。老师当场看完卷子后说:"你就先上三年级汉语班吧。"好强的我恳请老师能不能让我先上四年级汉语班试试,老师翻了翻卷子为难地说:"你看,这卷子除了小短文写得还可以,其他基础知识都答得不太好,连自己的名字都写错了吧,把赵晶颖的'赵'写成了'走'?"听了老师的话,我很不好意思,但最终还是坚持为自己争取到先上四年级汉语班试试的机会。此后,在剩余不多的暑期里,我把所有的时间都用在了补修汉语上,直到入校的前一天。

开学后,在新的学校的每一堂汉语课,我都集中精力地听讲,不停地给生字注音、注释,认真记笔记;回家后,写汉语作业,预习,不允许自己有丝毫马虎。渐渐地,我在汉语学习上的进步得到了老师们的认可,我也从"白字先生"成为了班里每次听写的第一二名;也从一个阅读课文时声音像蚊子似的没自信的学生变成班里的朗诵强将;还从一个写文章默默无闻的学生成为了班里的作文模范生。同时,我用汉语交流的能力也迅速提高,结交了更多的朋友。

五年级下半学期,我和父母商量要在五年级结束前参加汉语跳级考试,如果跳级成功,可以直接从四年级晋升到六年级汉语班。父母很赞成和支持我的想法,帮我买了五年级汉语教科书和练习册。我还向五年级的汉语老师——我的班主任——借了许多学习资料和优秀作文作为参考。就这样,我每天放学后，除了写四年级的汉语作业外，还要学习五年级的汉语教材，不懂的时候就求助老师和家人。那时我真的很少出去玩，更没时间看电视，有时看到楼下的小朋友们嬉笑玩耍，或看到大人们观看有趣的电视节目，心里十分羡慕。但我常常提醒自己：有得必有失，我的目标就是一定要争取通过汉语跳级考！

跳级考试那天终于到了，当我拿到试卷时，竟然丝毫没有感到紧张，与当初入学考试时的心态截然不同。我顺利地把卷子上的空格一一填满后，复查，交卷。老师当场判完后，笑着对我说："赵晶颖，真不错，你考了92分哦！开学后直接上六年级汉语班没问题。"我跳级成功啦！

我拿着那张用红笔写着92分的试卷在教室门口又蹦又跳，开心极了。真是功夫不负有心人啊！监考老师看着我兴奋的模样，开玩笑地说："赵晶颖，你记得吗？当初入学考试时，你连自己的名字都写错了，写成'走'晶颖了，看来在汉语学习上你是走着进来的，要飞着出去喽！"

的确，在那一刻，我高兴得真有一种想飞起来的感觉！

Learning Chinese At Beijing Fang Cao Di Elementary School

(Grade 7)

After fourth grade in Montessori, my parents decided to send me to the international section of a local elementary school—Fang Cao Di—for fifth and sixth grade in order to improve my Chinese. Unquestionably, it was a big challenge for me, as I had only studied in Montessori international schools since first grade. During the summer before the fifth grade, my mother made copies of the Chinese and math textbooks used in Fang Cao Di and assigned me homework to complete everyday in preparation for my entrance exam. Because there was a considerable difference between the math that I had learnt and the math that the local school taught, I mainly focused on catching up on that and thus I ended up not having an abundant[①] amount of time to thoroughly prepare for Chinese.

On the day of my entrance examination, I completed my math and English papers without much difficulty. For the last Chinese exam, I was absolutely stumped[②] when the teacher gave me my exam paper. I didn't know how to answer most of the questions; I nearly shed desperate tears. My examiner seemed to have observed how frantic[3] I was and came beside me to ask me whether I wanted to try the third grade level paper instead. I nodded automatically[4] and felt a sudden sense of anxiety, feeling extremely worried that I would also find the next paper too difficult. To my relief[5], when I got my paper, I realized I could answer more than half of the questions. I calmed down and concentrated on writing down all of the answers that I knew, but time was up before I was able to finish. I hurriedly wrote my name on the top right corner of my paper and handed it to the examiner for marking. After she had looked over it, she said: "I think it's best if you first go to third grade Chinese." I asked her whether she could reconsider and give me a chance to try studying in the fourth grade Chinese class at the beginning of the year. She flipped through my paper again, and replied with uncertainty[6]: "Well you see, apart from your short essay, all of the other questions on this paper were not answered that well, and I think you wrote your name wrong, am I right? You wrote your surname 'Zhao' into 'Zou' (the Chinese character for walking; if you add a cross to the character, it becomes the common surname 'Zhao')..." Realizing my foolish mistake, I was extremely embarrassed, but I still tried and eventually managed to convince the teacher to allow me to have a go at fourth grade Chinese. After that, with the aim of not being moved down to third grade Chinese, I began to work assiduously[7] to catch up in Chinese until the day before school began.

In my first Chinese class in Fang Cao Di, apart from listening attentively⑧ in class, I made sure I wrote down the pronunciation and definition of each Chinese character I did not know and took notes to revise at home. When I came back home, I spent a lot of time preparing for the next class and completing my Chinese homework thoroughly to avoid making unnecessary mistakes. As I continued to work hard, I began to earn recognition⑨ from my teachers. From a terrible speller, I became the student who always scored first or second in spelling quizzes; from a shy reader, I became the student who always volunteered to read aloud in class; and from the unnoticed new kid, I became a model student in essay writing in my Chinese class. At the same time, I found it much easier to express my thoughts when communicating with others, and began to make more new friends at school.

At the end of my first school term in fifth grade, I told my parents that I would like to skip a grade to sixth grade Chinese. My parents gave me full support and encouraged me to sign up for the exam at the end of the school year, and bought me the fifth grade Chinese textbook and exercise book. I also asked the current fifth grade Chinese teacher (my form tutor⑩) to lend me copies of some other materials their class had and would use and a selection of students' essays for good reference⑪ when I studied. And like this, everyday after coming home from school, I would first complete my fourth grade Chinese homework and then work on the fifth grade Chinese material, which I would ask my teacher and family for help with when I faced any problems. During that period, I hardly went out of the house to play or slump⑫ against the cushions on my couch and watch television. Whenever I saw children playing in the playground below my apartment or noticed my parents watching an interesting TV show, I would often feel very jealous, but I would always remind myself that in order to achieve my goal and pass the exam, I must pay a price, and that would mean sacrificing⑬ my free time.

The day for my "skipping a grade" exam finally arrived, and to my surprise, when I got my paper, I did not have the slightest feeling of uneasiness⑭, which was the complete opposite of how I felt during my entrance exam. I filled in all of the blanks on the test paper, double-checked my answers and handed in my paper. After the examiner had marked my paper, she gave me a reassuring smile: "Zhao Jing Ying, well done! You scored a ninety-two on this paper! When school starts, you can directly go to sixth grade Chinese." I had skipped to sixth grade Chinese!

I took my ninety-two mark test paper and bounced cheerfully to the door. All my hard work had finally paid off! The examiner looked at me and said jokingly: "Zhao Jing Ying, do you remember when you first came? You wrote your name into "Zou" JingYing on your entrance exam paper. I guess you really "walked" (zǒu) into this school, but will be "flying" out!"

At that moment, I was filled with joy, and found myself having a strong desire to take flight…

> 1 Abundant   adj.   丰富的，非常多的:She prepared an abundant supply of snacks for the long ride.
> 2 (Be) Stumped   v. (过去分词)难住；困住 :He was stumped by the last arithmetic question on the test.
> 3 Frantic   adj.   焦虑，焦急:The mother was frantic with worry.
> 4 Automatically   adv. 不禁地；自动的:"Yes," he replied automatically.
> 5 Relief   n.   放轻松，安心的状态:It was a great relief to the family that their son, Sam, came back home safely.
> 6 Uncertainty   n.   不确定的状态:She looked at me with great uncertainty.
> 7 Assiduously   adv.   刻苦地:You have to work assiduously in order to get into a good college.
> 8 Attentively   adv.   专注地:The students listened to the old man's speech attentively.
> 9 Recognition   n. 肯定:She has gained recognition for her outstanding literature works.
> 10 Form tutor   n.   班主任:Our form tutor handed out sign up slips for the trip.
> 11 Reference   n.   参考:He used many books from the library for reference when writing his report.
> 12 Slump   v. 驼着背地坐着或靠着:She slump [ed]（过去时) against the wall.
> 13 Sacrificing   v. (进行时)牺牲:Working hard should not lead to sacrificing your own health.
> 14 Uneasiness   n.   不自在，不安的状态:The employer became aware of the applicant's uneasiness by noticing how she constantly fidgeted with her fingers.

我心中的文学长官——文佩德

(初三)

参赛获奖作文(曾在北京市外籍中小学生汉语创作集《我喜欢汉语》内出版)

在世青中学的第一堂英语课,我满怀好奇地坐在了第一排讲台桌正下方的位置。上课铃刚响不久,蓝色的教室门开了,一位衣着休闲、身材高大的男士大步迈向讲台。他用那在浓眉下略带神秘的眼神环顾了一下周围,在黑板上醒目地写下了他的名字——文佩德。"同学们好,我叫文佩德,你们也可以叫我Peder,我将会在接下来的一年中担任你们的英语老师。"他带着大男孩似的微笑说。没穿皮鞋、没打领带,也没穿正式西装的他,让在座的同学们都感到略显紧张的气氛一下子缓和了许多。在他的自我介绍中得知,他是多伦多大学刚毕业不久的学生,才20多岁,没有什么教学经验。这让我们在座的很多同学在心中对这个老师是否能胜任英语教学画了一个大问号。但以后发生的事,使我们脑子里的疑问渐渐消失,进而对他产生了一种崇拜。

一天,文佩德先生在课上教了我们一篇文章。他把故事大致情节和文章所想表达的主题给我们整理了一遍后合上书,抬起头看了看我们,问:"你们认为这篇文章怎么样?"同学们相互看了看,不知如何回答才好。说实在的,那篇文章真没有什么出色的地方,主题也不突出,内容也不太吸引人,所以大家以沉默回应。对此,老师略显失望,干脆说:"我个人并不喜欢这篇文章。因为它用词平俗,内容也没有深度!"看到同学们诧异的表情,他停了下来,笑了笑,然后又接着说:"我相信许多同学也有同样的想法,但你们选择了沉默。记住,在我的课上,我喜欢一种真实,因为我希望你们成为文学评论家,自由地发表你们的看法。在语言的学习中,不但要学会积极地肯定和赞美,也要学会敢于质疑和批评。"就是从那一刻,我们对英语学习有了一种新鲜的感觉。每当我们进入这个教室,就会感到一种由衷的自信,因为在课堂上我们能毫无保留地发表自己的见解,并能得到老师的指导和肯定。

文佩德先生的授课内容是广泛的,除了文章他还会经常给我们讲一些生活中的趣事或读一两篇优秀的短文,作为课内的丰富与补充。

课后的文佩德先生风趣好动,常在篮球场上打球,跟同学们开玩笑,和学校里做杂工的阿姨们练中文。但在课上,他会变得严肃和认真。记得在我们的几次诗歌赏析课上,先生都会让同学们轮流朗诵,自己安静地坐在那里,时而略皱眉头,时而略带微笑,仔细地品味着同学们各异的朗诵风格,并给出自己的建议。有一天我突然发现,当不同语调,饱含着不同理解的声音充填那一张张写着诗文的书页时,我仿佛也进入了一个又一个富有意境的画面,陶醉在因文学的魅力而获得的幸福中。一次我坐在书桌前,突然有了一种写诗的冲动,提笔写了几句。之后经过反复练习,写诗逐渐成为了一种爱好。如今诗歌不仅是我观察事物的一种方式,也成为我以不同的视角发现和感悟事物内涵的一种文体。

初二期末,文佩德先生要离开学校了,他要去实现自己的梦想——当一名热衷于文学的旅游者。在他的最后一堂课上,吃完欢送蛋糕后,我们全班同学带着不舍和尊敬模仿了影片《死亡诗社》结尾的一段情节——大家都站在了一条长课桌上,从一数到三,齐声喊道:"长官,哦,长官!"那一刻大家都哭了,我们"长官"的眼睛也湿润了。那一刻我们永远都不会忘记。

如今已经初三的我,常常会想起初一、初二的英语班。文佩德先生给我们讲的趣闻趣事在同学之间还时常被提起,并依然会使我们像从前一样开怀大笑。跟先生学了近两年的英语,我不单单是提高了英语水平,还真正开始认识文学,喜爱文学,学会了用心去思考、去体会。文学不单单是书页上的字,它还可以有着如莎士比亚的浪漫、有着如简·奥斯丁的女权主义思想和有着如马克·吐温的风趣幽默。

翻开相册,凝视着我们全班和文佩德先生的合影,心里总会涌起一股暖流。先生依然笑得那么亲切,似乎还在给我们讲课。我由衷地希望先生的文学旅者之梦不再遥远。

MY CAPTAIN OF LITERATURE— PEDER VINGE

(Grade 9)

An Award—Winning Essay (published in "I Like Chinese"—a Chinese composition collection of expatriate students in Beijing)

When my first English class in junior high at Beijing World Youth Academy was about to begin, I chose a seat in the very front row that was right in front of the teacher's stand with a slight feeling of nervousness and excitement. Within a few seconds the bell rang, the blue classroom door suddenly swung open, and in came a broad figure casually dressed. He strolled up to the teacher's desk in large strides and used his pair of bright blue eyes below his thick brow for a quick scan across the room. He then spun smoothly towards the blackboard as he wrote his name in big capital letters: "Peder Vinge". "Hello class, my name is Peder Vinge or PR Star, I will be teaching you English this year," Mr. Vinge said with a childish smile. With the absence of the attire① of well-polished shoes, a straight tie and a tailor-made② suit, everyone loosened up③ a little. From his brief self-introduction, we learnt that he was a twenty-three year-old graduate from Toronto University and that this was his first year of teaching. This made us feel a certain doubt④ about his teaching abilities, but this sense of uncertainty quickly faded away as we gradually came to know him and it was replaced with pure gratitude⑤ and respect.

One time, Mr. Vinge briefly went through a short story in our textbooks. When he finished analyzing⑥ the main plot and idea of the story, he flipped the hard cover of his book and looked at us as he asked: "What did you guys think of the story?" We exchanged looks, not knowing how to answer the question. Honestly speaking, the short story was certainly not the finest of all, as it lacked a strong theme and appealing⑦ suspense⑧ in its plot. But everyone decided to hold back our critical⑨ tongues, as we were not sure how our teacher would respond. Mr. Vinge looked disappointedly towards the silent classroom and broke the awkwardness by saying firmly: "In my personal opinion, this short story was not a success. Its diction⑩ was bland⑪, its content⑫ lacked depth..." He stopped as he saw all of us staring at him in shock. He smiled: "I believe most of you may have thought similarly to me, but all of you chose to silence your thoughts. But I want you guys to become literary critics and voice your thoughts. When we study the English language, we should learn to appreciate while also having the courage to question and criticize, not compromise[13]."

It was from that moment that we changed our learning approaches in English. We felt that whenever we took a seat in this classroom, there was this sense of confidence which enabled[14] us to speak our thoughts and opinions unreservedly[15].

Mr. Vinge disliked his classes to be only based on knowledge from textbooks, so he would sometimes share personal anecdotes[16] with us or read one or two extracts of literature works from his own collection to enrich our language studies.

After class, we would always see Mr. Vinge in a baggy[17] basketball jersey out on the basketball court, joking around with younger students or learning Chinese with the ayis. But when he was in class, he became serious and taught with passion. I remember that during our poetry sessions, he would let us take turns to read a few stanzas as he sat quietly on his chair with his eyebrows sometimes knitted[18] together and other times relaxed into a grin. He listened to us attentively[19] and gave us suggestions when we finished our recitals. One day, I had a sudden feeling that when I listened to the different voices that delivered their own interpretation of the poem, the words printed on paper would instantly spring into life and appear as images in my mind. I was enchanted[20] with what could be achieved by the words of poetry. When I later sat at my desk, I had a sudden impulse to write a poem myself, and therefore jotted down a few lines. As I practiced writing more, I realized that composing poetry had gradually grown into a hobby. Poetry not only became a chance to observe, but also a form of writing in which I could experiment, contemplate[21] and learn to find aesthetic[22] qualities in ugly or even abominable[23] things by perceiving the world from different perspectives.

At the end of grade eight, Mr. Vinge told us that he was going to leave the school. He said that it would also be the end of his teaching career because he wishes to pursue his dream: to become a travel journalist. In our last class with Mr. Vinge, the whole class planned to reproduce[24] the ending scene of the movie 'The Dead Poet's Society'. After eating a goodbye cake, we all stood on our desks and shouted on the count of three: "My Captain, oh Captain!" The moment was mixed with tears and bitter smiles, and our captain also looked up at us with watery eyes. I believe that all of us will never be able to forget that moment.

Now, I am in Grade nine. I still often recall our English classes with Mr. Vinge in grade seven and eight. Those anecdotes that Mr. Peder shared with us are still shared amongst us from time to time, followed by familiar laughter. From my two years of English learning with Mr. Vinge, I not only improved my English skills in general but also began to become more familiar with and appreciate literature.

I realized that literature is not only just words; it could be romantic like William Shakespeare, feminist like Jane Austin or darkly humorous like Mark Twain…

As I flip through the pages of my photo album, I see pictures of our English class and our "Captain" as memories come up to me in a wave of warmth. In the pictures, our "Captain" is teaching to us and is still wearing his childish smile that will never fade away. I hope that he will carry this smile and our best wishes with him as he travels on the path towards his dream career.

1 Attire n. 衣着；穿着:His casual attire did not suit the occassion.

2 Tailor-made adj. （指衣服）定做的:All of his shirts and suits are tailor-made.

3 Loosened up v. （过去时）放轻松:His shoulder muscles loosened up as he exercised.

4 Doubt n. 置疑:She seems to be full of doubt.

5 Gratitude n. 感谢的心情:The old lady gave her neighbor a look of pure gratitude when he offered her a ride to town.

6 Analyzing v. （进行时）分析:During lunch, we saw Anna analyzing her data for her report.

7 Appealing adj. 吸引人的:Some people find life in the suburbs more appealing than living in the cities.

8 Suspense n. 悬念:The suspense in the book made its readers desperate to find out what happened next.

9 Critical adj. 批评的，挑剔的:Her frequent critical comments irritated many of her colleagues.

10 Diction n. 用词，措辞:In order to understand what the poet wishes to convey, we must pay attention to his or her diction.

11 Bland adj. 平庸，乏味:The taste of the food was

rather bland.

12 Content n. 内容:I enjoy his style of writing, but I dislike the content of this article.

13 Compromise v. 降低要求来接受:Vehicle companies cannot compromise on safety.

14 Enabled v.（过去时）使,能够:The huge amount of evidence that we managed to collect from weeks of research enabled us to win the debate.

15 Unreservedly adv. 毫无保留地:She unreservedly shared her most embarrassing moments to the class.

16 Anecdotes n. 小故事（通常是与自己有关的）:He included many anecdotes in his speech that amused his audience.

17 Baggy adj. 宽松的:Maria always wears baggy jeans.

18 Knitted v. 弄紧,编织（在这里指紧皱（眉头））:His eyebrows knitted together as he tried to remember his password for his online bank account.

19 Attentively adv. 专注地；集中精力地:The children listened attentively to their bedtime story.

20 (Be) Enchanted v.（过去分词）被迷惑,被吸引:She was absolutely enchanted with the new idea for the company's promotion.

21 Contemplate v. 思考；深思:The main idea conveyed in the story made her contemplate.

22 Aesthetic adj. 美丽的,有美感的:People may have different aesthetic principles, depending on their age, culture and the environment they live in.

23 Abominable adj. 令人讨厌的:The taste of the coffee was abominable.

24 Reproduce v. 复制；重新呈现:Andy Warhol's works have been commonly reproduc[ed]（过去分词）around the world.

2008年德威 Pop Idol

(高一)

我从世青中学转到德威国际学校时是2008年的1月初,刚上完9年级的上半学期。新学校对我来说无疑是一个全新和生疏的环境,除了要在短时间内掌握与前校截然不同的学习系统外,我最大的愿望是能尽快熟悉那些陌生的面孔。在入校大约4个月时,学校宣布要举办第一届德威"Pop Idol"歌唱比赛,而比赛的形式是模仿了美国很红的唱歌选拔赛——"American Idol[①]",将有3名老师分别扮演节目里的3位评委:Paula,Simon和Randy。几天之内,很多感兴趣的同学都把名字写在了音乐教室门外的报名表上。最初我很犹豫,但因为我确实很喜欢唱歌,同时也希望自己能通过参与这次活动让更多的同学认识我、了解我,我下决心去试一试。

海选地点被定在校内的小剧场。海选那天,为了不让自己过分紧张,在门口等待的我,两手堵住耳朵,小声地反复练习着准备参选的歌。当叫到我的名字时,我先让自己镇静了一下,慢慢地推开了剧场的门,只见4位老师坐在里面:3位评委和拿着摄影机的音乐老师。

看到摄影机,我心里哆嗦了一下,但很快用深呼吸缓解了一下紧张的情绪。我走到舞台中央,略带不自信地小声说:"我要演唱的是 The Wreckers 唱的一首歌,名叫《Cigarettes》。"评委们点点头,给了我一个开始的手势。

"Got my headlights shinin',down an old dirt road..."我边唱边用脚打着拍子。唱了一段,评委们叫我停下,在给了我一个比较肯定的点评后,被公众认为是最刻薄和挑剔的"Simon"问我:"你知道你在唱什么吗?"真够尖刻的,我心想。

当天下午,海选的结果在校会上公布。随着音乐老师把第一轮入选的名字一个个报出,台下便回应着一阵阵掌声和呼声。当老师最后念道:"Amy Zhao",我一时真不敢相信自己的耳朵,直到坐在我旁边的同学推了我一下,我才反应过来。

之后的选赛一路闯关,最终我竟然出乎意料地闯进了前12名,获得了参加决赛的资格。决赛定在"国际节"那天举行。竞赛规则是:12位选手演唱结束后,观众要往自己喜爱的选手前放置的号码桶里捐善款,以获捐的金额来决定名次。说心里话,能进决赛,我已经很知足了,不奢望自己能胜出,但还是希望能通过自己力所能及的方式筹到更多的善款。

"国际节"终于到了。那天晚上 Battle of the Bands(摇滚乐队之间的比赛)结束后,12个Pop Idol的选手被叫到台边做准备,我被排到第10位。听到前几位参赛者的演唱,我开始有了压力,因为他们的确都唱得很好,宽广的音域,响亮的声音,让我羡慕不已。但我不停地提醒自己要放松,要用心去唱,唱出自己的特点。

"现在让我们掌声有请Amy Zao上台!"话音一落,我快步走上台,向观众鞠了个躬。

"我把你的名字说对了吗?是Zao吗?"音乐老师突然问。

"不是'Zao',是'Zhao'。"

"那你先下去,我再重叫一遍。"他风趣地说。

神奇的是,当我第二次被叫上台时,紧张感似乎消失了。我手握麦克风,轻松地说:"女士们、先生们、同学们和老师们,大家晚上好。我要演唱的歌曲是The Wreckers唱的一首乡村歌曲《Cigarettes》,希望你们喜欢。"说完,我忽然感觉整个舞台都是我的。

音乐响起,我随着音乐唱了起来:"Got my headlights shinin',down an old dirt road...",唱着唱着,我完全进入状态,情感与歌曲融为一体,边唱边随着旋律舞动着。台下的观众们也兴奋地跟着节奏摆动着双手!当我尽情地唱完时,热烈的掌声和欢呼声让我感到无比的兴奋和满足!

演唱结束后,投票的时间到了。在大家上前为自己喜爱的表演者投票时,我们12位参赛者又被叫上台去一起演唱

U2 的一首《I Still Haven't Found What I'm Looking For》。演唱的过程中,不少人走到我的面前,把善款投入桶内。还有些同学不仅投给了自己的朋友,同时也投给了我,这是对我的一种肯定,使我心存感激。

最终统计结果出来了,写着结果的纸被递到音乐老师手里。他宣布了第三名和第二名后,大声地说道:"——第一名——Amy Zhao!"当时我真的呆住了!那个时刻,那个让我差一点儿就要大叫和流泪的时刻使我终生难忘!我又一次被叫上台,惊喜地接过自己本没想到属于自己的奖杯,激动得一句话也说不出来。音乐老师指着我肩上的背包开玩笑地说:"看来你不准备等结果就要回家喽!"真的,那一天是我有生以来最最开心和兴奋的一天。虽然我从小就参加过各种比赛,也拿过不少的奖,可这一次不同,因为实在是太意外了,正因为此,那种喜悦是由衷的、深刻的,是难以形容的。

大赛结束后,我再也不是大家都陌生的新生,而是第一届德威 Pop Idol 的获奖者——Amy Zhao。更重要的是,通过参加这次活动,我进一步坚定了要把握各种机会和拿出足够的勇气去挑战的决心,因为每一次机会和挑战,都包藏着无限有益的因素,那是我们在课程之外的又一门必修课。

再次感谢新校——德威给了我们这个擦亮青春的机会。

Dulwich Pop Idol of 2008

(Grade 10)

I changed schools from Beijing World Youth Academy to Dulwich College Beijing in January 2008, after my first school term in grade nine. The school was a whole new experience for me; apart from the need to adapt to a different educational system, I knew that I also had to meet and befriend a new group people. After four months in my new school, there was an announcement saying that the school would be holding a whole new singing competition called the 'Dulwich Pop Idol', which was a reproduction of the famous 'American Idol' show in the States, and three teachers would act as the three judges, Paula, Simon and Randy, in the show. Sign-up sheets for auditions were stuck outside the music room, and began to fill up with names very quickly. At first, I was hesitant to sign up, but because I really loved singing and wished that I could use this opportunity to get more involved in the school and get more people to know me, I decided to take the chance.

Auditions were held in the school theatre. On the day of my audition, I tried to reduce my nervousness while waiting by the doors of the theatre with fingers stuffed in my ears as I quietly practiced my song. When my name was called, I calmed myself down and slowly opened the door. There were only four teachers inside: the three judges and our music teacher at the side holding a video camera. Seeing the video camera made me shake a little but I managed to loosen up a bit by taking a big breath. I walked to the middle of the stage as I said hesitantly: "I am going to perform a song by The Wre- Wreckers. It's called 'Cigarettes'." The judges nodded and gave me a hand gesture[①] to tell me to begin.

"Got my headlights shinin', down an old dirt road..." I sang while tapping my right foot. The judges stopped me halfway through the chorus and gave me some positive comments. The only criticism that the notorious "Simon" gave me was: "Do you understand what you're singing about?", which was quite harsh.

On the same day, the results were to be announced in our weekly assembly. Our music teacher read out the names of the people who had entered the first round as others cheered and applauded. When at last he read out "...and Amy Zhao", I couldn't believe my ears and did not react until one of my classmates poked me in the side.

After that, I unexpectedly got to the top twelve finalists, and was to perform and compete on International Day. The winner was to be voted for by the audience donating money in the bucket with the number of their favorite contestant[②] stuck on it. All of the money was to go to charity.

Honestly speaking, I was already more than happy to be able to enter the finals, and did not think that I had a chance of winning, but I did wish that I could use my voice to raise more money for charity. Because it was a month before our internal exams, I did not have enough time to prepare a new song, so I decided to stick with "Cigarettes" for the final competition.

International Day finally arrived. After the Battle of the Bands (a competition between the rock bands in our school), the twelve Pop Idol contestants were called beside the stage to get ready. According to the order, my performance was tenth in line. After I had heard the first few contestants sing, I began to feel the pressure; they were all very talented and quite a few of them had a higher and better voice than I did. I kept on telling myself to relax and believe in my abilities, and that I was to sing from the heart, with emotion and passion. "Now let's give a hand to Amy Zao on stage!" my music teacher said. I hastily[3] walked up the stairs and bowed to the audience.

"Did I say your name right? Is it Zao?" my music teacher suddenly asked.

"It's 'Zhao', not 'Zao'."

"Oh, then go off stage, let me call you up again," he said humorously[4]. Surprisingly, when I stepped on stage for the second time, my fears and nervousness seemed to have disappeared. I held the microphone as I spoke with ease: "Good evening ladies and gentlemen, students and teachers. Now I am going to perform a country song by The Wreckers called "Cigarettes", hope you all enjoy."

After that, I felt like the stage was mine. The music started, and I began to sing: "Got my headlights shinin', down an old dirt road..." As I sang, I got more and more into the song and started to move with the beat. I could slightly see the audience also swaying[5] with the rhythm and waving their hands up in the air... When I finished the song, I was thrilled[6] to hear people applauding and cheering loudly for me as I bowed again.

After everyone had performed, it was time for the voting. While people dropped their money into the buckets, all of the twelve contestants were called on stage again to perform "I Still Haven't Found What I'm Looking For" by U2. During our group performance, I saw quite a few unfamiliar faces drop money into my bucket. There were also students that not only voted for their friends, but also voted for me. I was really touched and felt a sense of reward, as it showed their recognition of my performance.

The results finally came out, and a white piece of paper was passed into the hands of my music teacher as he began to read out the final results. After he had announced the third and second place, he said loudly: "...and the winner is... Amy Zhao!"

I was completely dumbstruck[7]. I don't think I will ever be able to forget that moment, when I almost screamed in excitement and burst into happy tears. I went up onto the stage once again to collect my trophy in huge shock, unable to speak. My music teacher pointed at my bag hung on my shoulder as he said jokingly: "Looks like you were all ready to leave before the results came out!" I have to say, it was one of the happiest moments that I have ever had. I have attended many other competitions before, but this was different because from the very beginning, I did not have a glimpse of a thought that I would win. It is a magical feeling when you get something that you have never expected to get.

After that night, I was no longer the new girl without a name, but the first Pop Idol winner, Amy Zhao. And most of all, the experience further confirmed my belief that we should learn to grasp⑧ opportunities that come by and have the courage to 'go for it', because they can act as a platform⑨ to exhibit your talents, develop your confidence and explore your self-worth. Here, I would like to thank my new school, Dulwich College Beijing, again, for this valuable opportunity.

---

1 Gesture n. 手势:The conductor made a gesture for the orchestra to sit down.

2 Contestant n. 参赛者:Many contestants in this competition are from England.

3 Hastily adv. 匆忙地:She hastily changed into her office clothes, as she was late for work.

4 Humorously adv. 幽默,风趣地:The two brothers talked about their sister humorously.

5 Swaying v. (进行时)摇摆,摆动:The willows sway[ed] (过去式) gently with the wind.

6 (Be) Thrilled v. (过去分词)激动:The mother was thrilled to see her children back.

7 Dumbstruck adj. 惊呆;被惊喜得发愣:The crowd was absolutely dumbstruck when Mary started to sing.

8 Grasp v. 把握:You will begin to grasp the concept as you practice.

9 Platform n. 平台:All of the performers stood on the concert platform for the big finale.

II.
CULTURAL TRIPS...
文化体验

1999
WINTER,
IN THE
UNITED
STATES
OF
AMERICA

一九九九年 冬，
美国

北京城的奥运之旅

(高一)

2001年7月13日,一个令人难忘的日子,是我的,更是全中国人民的。

那天晚上,我和家人守在电视机前,观看2008年申奥结果宣布的直播。当奥委会主席萨马兰奇宣布:"Beijing! China!"那一刻,我兴奋地从沙发上蹦了起来,不由自主地喊着:"是北京!北京!北京!"虽然当年5月份,我刚刚从加拿大回到北京,但我似乎对这个城市有一种自然而亲切的情感。那一夜,年仅8岁的我和全中国人民一起欢呼雀跃,整个北京城都沸腾了!

申奥成功后,北京开始加速了发展步伐:从现代化建筑的拔地而起到名胜古迹的维修和保护;从对空气质量的关注到植树造林环保绿化的落实;从提高全民的文明素质的呼吁到老百姓自发地学习英语,这一切都让我感受到了奥运的精神和理念已渐渐渗进这个城市。就拿我居住的小区来说:违章的建筑被拆除了,垃圾和异味消失了,凹凸不平的道路不见了,取而代之的是新建的居民区、洁净平坦的路面、美味的中西餐厅和方便的超市,还有那一群群各种肤色的人们在露天咖啡厅欢笑交谈的情景。北京的开放和包容刷新了我对这个城市的印象。

在北京筹备奥运会的后半阶段,变化更是日新月异。从2005年开始,北京市解除了春节烟花爆竹的禁放令。每当中国传统的庆典——农历新年来临时,从除夕夜开始,人们可以连续不断地享受到北京夜空的烟花盛宴。那多姿多彩的烟花,震耳欲聋的爆竹声,让我深感到一种传统文化的回归和这个城市巨大的爆发力。而每当我观赏到这种在世界上绝无仅有的被烟花浸染的绚丽夜空时,都有一种震撼和感触,它仿佛拉响了奥运会的前奏曲!此外,随着奥运会的临近,北京城处处可见奥运会开幕式的倒计时牌,看着它一分一秒的变动,让我的内心涌动着想为奥运会做些什么的冲动。我到处查询如何能成为一名奥运会志愿者,也曾准备报名考试,但由于不满18岁,未能如愿。但最终在母亲的帮助下,我有机会在一个奥运指定医疗机构当了一名非正式志愿者,用我的语言特长在诊所的前台为奥运健儿们的就医尽了一份微薄之力。

2008年8月8日,北京奥运会终于在举世瞩目的开幕式下拉开帷幕。开幕式的整台表演像是北京这几年来向全世界交出的一份答卷,它以缤纷夺目的礼花为序言,以悠久的中国历史文化为基调,用美轮美奂的灯光,精湛独特的表演和扣人心弦的奥运点火仪式,向全世界展现了中华文化的精彩和中华民族的智慧。

奥运会期间,我每天都迫不及待地想亲临奥运赛场观战。终于有一天,我和父母乘地铁来到了奥林匹克公园,准备去水立方观看男子跳水半决赛。阳光下的奥运主场馆——鸟巢和水立方傲立在公园内,十分壮观。银蓝色的水立方外壁上映着对面鸟巢的倩影,使我按动相机快门的手停不下来。

比赛开始前,我走进水立方,场馆内现代化的设施让我大开眼界,充满紧张气氛的赛事更让我兴奋不已。各国奥运健儿们优美的高难度跳水动作给我留下了难忘的印象。

比赛结束后,当我走出场馆,原本是银蓝色的水立方在夜幕下变成了变幻多姿的"水魔方",五彩缤纷、耀眼迷人。而对面的鸟巢,此时在灯光下,是透明的艳红色,就像是一整块红水晶被一层层金属条环绕着,晶莹剔透,充满着艺术气息。鸟巢上方的奥运火炬依然伫立,熊熊燃烧。此时,在场的国人们、各国的游客们和我一样在这美景下流连忘返,都想从不同角度把这画面存入脑海、拍入胶片。

奥运会终于众望所归,成功闭幕了。从申奥成功到奥运会结束,我似乎经历了7年的奥运旅程。从奥运可以看到很多人类共同的追求:生命,强健,对人的潜能的探寻;艺术,美善,基于平等的和平与企盼。我很幸运地见证了北京这一具有里程碑意义的时刻,它将一个前进中的城市托举在世界面前。

THE 2008 BEIJING OLYMPICS

(Grade 10)

July 13th, 2001, is a day that I, and the whole population of China, will never forget.

That night, my whole family crowded round the TV screen, watching the 2008 Olympic games host announcement live. When the former president of the International Olympic Committee, Juan Antonio Samaranch, announced, "Beijing! China! " I sprung from my sofa and shouted repeatedly and gleefully①: "It's Beijing! Beijing! Beijing! ..." Although I had only moved to Beijing from Canada in May that year, I somehow felt a natural bond② with the city. As a seven-year-old girl, I cheered along with China and its people; that night, Beijing was filled with energy.

After it was announced that Beijing had won the Olympic bid, the city began to increase its pace③ of development: from the modernized④ architecture to the restoration⑤ and rejuvenation⑥ of historical buildings and sites; from improved air quality to the effort put in for a better and greener environment; and from the awareness of the need for a more cultured society to an increasing number of the population desirous to learn English, I strongly felt that the Olympics had greatly driven Beijing's enthusiasm towards its development. Evident⑦ changes had also been made in my residential area: abandoned⑧ buildings were torn down; trash and a pervasive⑨, lingering stench⑩ and uneven roads gradually disappeared. In their place were new urban⑪ residential areas, better and smoother roads, delicious restaurants, convenient⑫ shops and increasing groups of foreigners comfortably lounging⑬ in outdoor cafés … All of these changes created a more pleasant and contemporary⑭ atmosphere that renewed my impression of the city.

During Beijing's later development and preparation for the Olympics, further changes were made. In the year 2005, the government decided to remove the firework ban⑮ during Chinese New Years in Beijing. Thus, when the traditional festival arrived, the whole city was able to watch and enjoy the night sky filled with the bloom of spectacular⑯ fireworks. The vibrant⑰ fire flowers and the loud and constant bang of firecrackers were reminiscent of days gone by as well as reflecting the city's immense⑱ potential⑲ and energy. And whenever I admired these exceptional⑳ firework celebrations, I would wonder in astonishment, seeing it as a prelude㉑ to the upcoming Olympics... As the Games drew even closer, countdown boards for the Opening Ceremony popped up everywhere in Beijing. Whenever I saw the numbers change on the digital board, a sudden craving[22] to make some kind of contribution[23] to the Olympics would surge within me. As a result, I began to search and inquire[24] into how to become an Olympic volunteer, and prepared to register and take the required exam, but was eventually turned down[25] because I did not fulfill the eighteen-year-old age requirement. Nevertheless, with the help of my mother, I was able to volunteer at a clinic assigned to provide services for athletes and important visitors during the Olympics, and I made use of my linguistic[26] abilities to offer help at the reception.

On August 8th, 2008, the Beijing Olympics finally began with an astounding Opening Ceremony that impressed its worldwide audience. The entire stage seemed to officially display to the world Beijing's progression over the past few years. Following the burst of magnificent fireworks, the ceremony began with a strong cultural tone, filled with exciting lights and lavish[27] performances, and finally concluded with a novel[28] torch lighting ceremony, showcasing[29] the essence[30] of China's rich culture and its capital's unique[31] character.

During the Olympics, as I volunteered at the international clinic and kept track of the games and results through different media sources, I felt an increasing desire to go and watch from inside the actual stadium. The day finally arrived and my parents and I took the subway to the Olympic Green to watch the men's springboard semi-final at the Water Cube. Under the hot summer sun, the main Olympic stadiums, the Bird's Nest and the Water Cube stood confidently㉜ inside the park, attracting the eyes of tourists. I was fascinated to see the Water Cube's silvery blue exterior reflect the image of the Bird's Nest located across the road, and I found myself unable to put down my camera as I tried to take pictures of everything I saw. Before the game started, I stepped inside the Water Cube, surprised by its modern interior, and was overwhelmed with excitement. During the match, the challenging diving movements that the divers beautifully performed left a great impression on me.

When the semi-final was over, I walked out, and found that the silvery blue Aquatics Center had transformed into a mesmerizing color-changing cube. As I looked towards the Bird's Nest, red lights glowed beneath its steel structure, making it seem somewhat like a glowing red gem carefully entwined㉝ with layers of metal wires, enhancing㉞ the night with its artistic touch. On the very top of the stadium, the Olympic torch still roared with an energetic flame. I saw that all of the local Chinese and foreign visitors were, like me, lingering㉟ in the park, unwilling to leave, trying to capture this view with eager eyes and cameras to keep it in their memory.

The Olympics was finally brought to an end with its Closing Ceremony. From the day that Beijing won its Olympic bid to the grand finale, I felt like I had gone through a seven-year Olympic tour. The Olympics seemed to have demonstrated many of our human values such as: life, health, the search to reach our own potential; and benevolence, equality and the hope for peace... I am fortunate to have had the chance to witness[⑤] first-hand Beijing's development and how it distinguished itself to the world with its progression and evident potential.

> 1 Gleefully adv. 十分开心地:She skipped gleefully on the grass plain.
> 2 Bond n. 关联；紧密的联系:There are very strong bonds between each member of this team; they are like a family.
> 3 Pace n. 速度；步伐:The town has developed at an incredibly fast pace over the past few years.
> 4 Modernized adj. 现代化的:New modernized buildings are gradually being built.
> 5 Restoration n. 修复的过程:The town needs a lot of money for its restoration.
> 6 Rejuvenation n. 更新或复原的过程:Citizens are bidding for the authorities to provide more financial support for the town's rejuvenation project.
> 7 Evident adj. 明显的:It is evident that the plan is not very efficient.
> 8 Abandoned adj. 被抛弃的，无人居住的:Most of the abandoned houses down this street have been vandalized.
> 9 Pervasive adj. 弥漫的:There is a pervasive smell of cigarette smoke in her living room.
> 10 Stench n. 臭气，恶臭:The sewer gave out a terrible stench.
> 11 Urban adj. 城市的:Urban residents are generally wealthier than those who live in rural areas.
> 12 Convenient adj. 方便的:The new subway line has made it much more convenient for me to go to work.

13 Lounging v. (进行时)懒洋洋地坐着:She loung[ed] (过去时)around in pajamas.

14 Contemporary adj. 当代的，现代的:The gallery exhibited many contemporary artworks.

15 Ban n. 禁止，禁令:Several proposals have been made to ban smoking in public.

16 Spectacular adj. 壮观的:You can enjoy a spectacular view of the whole city from the peak.

17 Vibrant adj. 明亮的；生机勃勃的:The vibrant colors of this painting really catch the eye.

18 Immense adj. 巨大的:The immense auditorium impressed its visitors.

19 Potential n. 潜力:She has great potential in broadcasting.

20 Exceptional adj. 特别的；稀有的:There is an exceptional view on the top of this mountain.

21 Prelude n. 序；前奏:The wonderful performances were a prelude to the sumptuous banquet.

22 Craving n. 渴望:She had a sudden craving for strawberry cheesecake.

23 Contribution n. 贡献:She is known for her many contributions to charity.

24 Inquire v. 查询，询问:She inquir[ed] about application dates at the reception.

25 Turned down v. (过去时)被拒绝:He was turned down by the admissions office.

26 Linguistic adj. 语言方面的:Maria won the job due to her outstanding linguistic abilities.

27 Lavish adj. 奢华的:He treated his visitors to a lavish banquet.

28 Novel adj. 新颖的；新奇的:A novel idea suddenly came across his mind.

29 Showcasing v. 展示:Gary's presentation showcas[ed] (过去时) his talents and the tremendous effort he had put into his project.

30 Essence n. 本质，精髓:Conflict is the essence of drama.

31 Unique adj. 独特的:The unique designs of the new collection earned much praise from various influential fashion critics.

32 Confidently adv. 自信地:She walked confidently into the classroom.

33 Entwined v.（过去时）缠住,盘绕:The house was entwined in ivy.

34 Enhancing v. 提高:Nowadays, many people use computer programs to enhance photo quality.

35 Lingering v. 徘徊:He linger[ed](过去时) at the door.

36 Witness v. 亲眼看见,目睹:The police questioned the salesman who witness[ed](过去时) the incident.

加拿大魁北克市游记

(初一)

1998年的夏天,我和父母第一次来到了加拿大的法语城市——魁北克。这是一座可亲而古朴的城市,一间间欧式小屋和一座座法式餐厅排列在道路两旁,配上柔和的灯光,比起大气的北美城市,这里多了几分小巧和温馨。

到达的当晚,我们来到了一家小有名气的法式餐厅。拿到菜单时,我发现上面写的都是法文。学了一些法语的我,顿时来了精神,想在不会法语的父母面前露一手。于是,我尽力地给父母翻译那些我看得懂的菜名。点菜时,我试着用法语把一道道菜名念出来。也许惊异于看到一个亚洲脸的孩子会讲法语,服务员也开心地用简单的法语和我交流。当时,我感到自豪极了。

环顾四周,我发现几乎每个用餐的人都在喝红葡萄酒,边喝边细细地品尝菜肴,其中大部分的人都在讲法语。同在加拿大,这里却与我居住的多伦多市相差甚远,那里的人都讲英语,吃饭的速度也很快。

这顿饭我不仅吃得开心,还让我体验到了在北美大环境中的一种欧式风情,更更重要的是,它增加了我对语言学习的浓厚兴趣。

第二天下午,观光了大半天后,我们在一条小街旁的露天咖啡厅坐下休息,父母各自点了一杯咖啡,而我则喝着饮料,看着过往的行人和古式马车。在暖阳下,我渐渐有了一些睡意。这时,一位玩杂耍的青年男子的出现,使我睡意顿消。他一边骑着单轮车,一边轻松地耍着3个塑料保龄球瓶,笑容满面。我快速地迎上前去,想看个究竟。他看到我,忽然停了下来,向我招招手,并递给我3个保龄球瓶,问我要不要试着耍一耍。我点点头,拿起瓶子就向空中扔,结果一个都没有接着。我不好意思地连忙把瓶子捡起来还给他,说了一句:"Excusez-moi(请原谅)!"他笑了笑,在夸奖了我的勇气后,幽默而夸张地模仿了我刚才的那一幕,我们一起哈哈大笑了起来。不知何时赶过来的父母,用相机拍下了这精彩的一瞬间。杂耍青年向我们挥挥手,坐上了单轮车,一边骑一边又欢快地耍起了瓶子。我还依依不舍地站在那里,看着这个带给大家欢乐的青年,在人群中渐渐远去。

魁北克这个坐落在北美大地的小城,它那古朴沉静的街道,热情风趣的人们,精致美味的菜肴和多种文化和语言的环境,使我对这个坐落在北美大地的法式小城情有独钟。

QUEBEC CITY, CANADA

(Grade 7)

In the summer of 1998, my parents and I visited Canada's French-speaking city—Quebec City. It was filled with a sense of amiability① and elegance: small European-style housing and French restaurants sat along both sides of its streets, with strings of decorative lights that harmonized② with the environment. Compared to the usual North American ambiance, this place seemed more delicate and refined.

On the night of our arrival, we went to a well-known French restaurant for dinner. When we received the menu, I realized that everything was written in French. As I had studied some French in school, I was delighted, and thought that it was a great opportunity for me to show off some of my skills to my parents who were then looking blankly③ at the menu. Thus, I tried my best to translate the names of the dishes that I could read for them. After I raised my hand to call a waitress, I read out our order slowly and carefully. The waitress, who seemed to be surprised to see an Asian child speaking French, began to communicate with me enthusiastically, which filled me with a sense of pride. As I looked around, I observed that nearly everyone dining in the restaurant had a glass of wine placed beside their dish, and took a few sips from time to time as they savored[④] their meal and chattered in French. Although the place was also situated in Canada, it was very different from Toronto (where I lived back then), where people spoke English and ate in big bites.

Apart from enjoying a delicious meal and experiencing a lively European—style atmosphere, I also found myself becoming more interested in language studies.

On the following day, after sightseeing the whole morning, we stopped to rest at an outdoor café by a small road. My parents both ordered a cup of coffee while I sipped my drink and watched pedestrians[⑤] and horse-drawn carriages[⑥] pass by. Under the warm afternoon sun, I began to doze[⑦] off, but instantly snapped[⑧] back to life as an image in front of me caught my eye: a cheerful young juggler riding along the road on his unicycle[⑨] while skillfully[⑩] juggling[⑪] three plastic bowling pins. Fascinated, I jumped to my feet and quickly ran towards him for a closer look. Noticing my approach, he suddenly stopped cycling, waved at me and passed me his three bowling pins while asking me whether I would like to try juggling them. I nodded my head, received the three bowling pins and threw them in the air, but to my embarrassment, none of them fell back into my hands. I hurriedly picked up all of the pins from the ground and handed them back to him as I said, "Excusez-moi (please forgive me)!" He smiled, complimented my courage, and then humorously and exaggeratedly[12] imitated[13] my juggling attempt, which left both of us in hysterical[14] laughter. My parents, who suddenly appeared beside us, took a picture of this unforgettable moment. The young juggler then waved at us, rode on his bicycle, and began to juggle happily again. I stood there, wishing that he could stay a bit longer, and watched him slowly disappear into the crowd...

During my few days in Quebec City, its charming[15] streets, welcoming and lightly humorous citizens, appetizing food and multi-cultural and bilingual environment completely drew me towards this North American French city and left me reminiscing[16] about its beauty.

---

1 Amiability n. 和蔼,可亲: Her amiability made people feel comfortable around her.

2 Harmonized v. (过去时)调和,融洽: The red flowers harmonize(现在时) with the colors of the room.

3 Blankly adv. 茫然地: She stared blankly at her test paper.

4 Savored v. 细细品尝: The family savored their appetizing dinner.

5 Pedestrians n. (复数)行人: This road only allows pedestrians.

6 Horse Carriages n. (复数)马车: Before the invention of cars, rich people travelled on horse-drawn carriages.

7 Doze v. 昏昏沉沉;打盹儿: He was so exhausted that he doz[ed](过去时) off in class.

8 Snapped v. (过去时)忽然振作或唤醒: She snapped

back to reality from her daydream when the teacher tapped on her desk.

9 Unicycle n. 单轮车:Jimmy got a unicycle for his birthday.

10 Skillfully adv. 有技巧地:He made use of propaganda skillfully to win support for the election.

11 Juggling v. （进行时）玩杂耍:She is juggling five apples.

12 Exaggeratedly adv. 夸张地:She performed exaggeratedly on stage.

13 Imitated v.(过去时)、模仿、仿效:She was annoyed at her older brothers for imitat[ing](进行时)her.

14 Hysterical adj. 控制不住的，不停地:The singer's bodyguards protected her from hysterical fans.

15 Charming adj. 迷人的:She has a charming smile.

16 Reminiscing v. 追忆:He sat in his rocking chair, reminiscing about his past.

美国游记

(初三)

1999年的冬天,也就是我6岁那年,我们一家三口从加拿大随旅行团去美国西部旅游。这是我第一次踏上享有世界最发达国家之称的土地,充满好奇心的我对这次旅行充满了期待。

我们最先来到的地方是加利福尼亚州,给我印象最深的是好莱坞的环球影城。去影城的当天,排了一段很长的队后,我们被带到了一个银白色的电梯内,乘着电梯来到了一间摆放着一辆红色跑车的宽敞的房间里。游客们纷纷进入车座,系上安全带后,屋里顿时变得漆黑,眼前却突然出现了一座座火山和紧跟着我们的恐龙。我惊奇地瞪着双眼,看着这一切,享受着冒险的刺激。直到结束,我才从逼真的虚拟世界中回到了现实,发现我们依然在那个大房间里,而红色的跑车也在原地纹丝未动。这时,我才真正醒悟过来,原来整个效果都是靠一个三维的大屏幕和车身精确的摆动配合而成的,令我叹为观止。由于游客实在太多,我们只玩了4种,但这足以使我见识美国科技的高度发达,带给年幼的我以强烈的感官冲击。

离开好莱坞影城,我们来到了世界大宝藏之一——赫式堡观光。沿着风景壮观的盘山路,驱车来到了这个坐落在云山之中的梦幻城堡。从进入这座既带有欧洲的典雅,又融入了北美自然舒放格调的城堡的那一刻,我就很羡慕在这里生活过的主人——赫斯特,想像他一定是一位由衷地热爱自然和艺术的绅士。

城堡周围有许多精雕细刻的塑像和华丽的大理石台阶,而城堡里的艺术品更是精美绝伦,数不胜数。至今,我还常常会梦见城堡里的室内游泳池。当时导游介绍,游泳池名叫罗马池,我们脚下所踩的地面是用威尼斯制造的马赛克玻璃拼贴而成的,上面还贴了一层薄薄的黄金。走在那华丽耀眼的泳池地面上,我的脚步自动地放慢、放轻,生怕破坏了它的美。

从这个城堡的每一个角落,都能看得出主人赫斯特在上面所倾注的心血,而里外的所有结构装饰都反映了他那丰富的想象力和浪漫情结。在城堡的瞭望台放眼望去,阳光下一片泛着点点波光的碧海和周围连绵的山脉,与天空的朵朵白云融为一体,壮美诱人。我想,赫斯特当初建筑城堡的设想大概是由此景而生的吧!

旅程的最后一站是拥有世界娱乐首都之称的拉斯维加斯。飞机在傍晚到达,虽然当时我发着烧,但拉斯维加斯的夜晚令身体的不适暂时消失了。绚丽的灯光,热闹的人群,让我目不暇接。形状各异的宾馆鳞次栉比，步入任何一个宾馆的大厅，都能感觉到缭绕的烟雾，看到赌博的人们各异的神情，听到老虎机吞吐钱币的声音。拉斯维加斯是一个聚财的世界，一个享受的世界，也许还是一个追梦的世界。它的缤纷色彩和歌舞升平令我眼花缭乱。回到宾馆，我浑身就像散了架一样倒头就睡，也许只有在这种状态下才能感受到这座城市的一种安静吧。

初次的美国之旅确实使我大开眼界，它的现代化，它的美丽，它的热情和活力都深深吸引了我，成为了我心中的梦之国。

THE UNITED STATES

(Grade 9)

In the winter of 1998, when I was six, my parents and I went on a tour around the west of the United States from Canada. It was the first time I had stepped foot in one of the most influential and developed countries in the world, and as a child, I was filled with curiosity and wonder.

The first state that we visited was California, and what left the biggest impression on me was Universal Studios in Hollywood. On the day that we visited the amusement park, we queued up for a long time until we were allowed to enter a silver elevator to be taken up to a spacious[①] room with a smart red sports car in the middle. After everyone had taken a seat in the car and fastened[②] his or her seatbelt, the lights in the room suddenly went off, and we instantly found ourselves in a land of volcanoes with a hungry dinosaur chasing after us. I watched everything that happened in front of me with my eyes wide open, experiencing the ultimate thrill of this exciting adventure. Only when it was over did I finally come back to reality from the virtual world and comprehend③ that we were still in the exact same room and the red sports car had not moved an inch. It was then that I truly realized that the gripping④ visual effect was entirely created by a three-dimensional ⑤ screen and the corresponding accurate movement of the car. Because there were too many people in the park, we only had time to go on four rides, but they were enough to leave me in complete awe⑥.

After we had set off from Hollywood, we began our road trip to Hearst Castle——one of the world's most expensive properties. Spiraling⑦ up the road to the top of San Simeon, we arrived at the dream castle built in enchanting scenery. From the very moment I entered this castle of European sophistication ⑧ and North American grandeur⑨, I admired its owner, William Randolph Hearst, for having owned such a fortune, and presumed that he must have been a fine gentleman who was enamored⑩ of nature and art.

Many beautifully carved sculptures and elegant marble staircases surrounded the castle's exterior, while inside, the castle was filled with valuable antiques. Yet, what I still dream of is its indoor swimming pool, which left a permanent imprint⑪ on my memory. From our tour guide's introduction, I learnt that the name of the pool was the Roman Pool, and the floor that we were then stepping on consisted of smalti⑫ tiles from the city of Venice, fused⑬ with gold. As I walked on this delicate piece of luxurious art, my footsteps became instinctively slower and lighter, as I felt slightly scared that I would damage its beauty.

Not a single aspect of this castle failed to reflect the huge amount of effort that Hearst had put in, and from its construction and internal[14] decoration and design, I could perceive that he was an imaginative and romantic man. Standing from one point in the castle grounds, I looked out towards the blue-green sea glistening[15] under the shining sun, the chain of gentle hills and slopes surrounding it and the plump white clouds hanging in a lively way above them; the entire picture was a marvel[16]. I believe that Hearst's initiative[17] to build this castle on San Simeon must have been inspired by its breathtaking[18] scenery.

Our last stop of the tour was the "Entertainment Capital of the World"—Las Vegas. Our airplane arrived at dawn, and I had developed a high fever from the tour, but Las Vegas' fascinating nightlife made me forget that I was feeling unwell. The flamboyant[19] lights and groups of loud, energetic[20] people seemed almost too much for me to take in all at once. Hotels of different shapes and designs stood next to each other along the busy streets and the lobby of each one we visited was filled with smoke, eager and anxious gamblers and the sound of slot machines generously eating up and spitting out money... From what I saw, I felt that Las Vegas was a city where cash piled up in stacks; where people sought entertainment and excitement and where people hoped for a second chance to fulfill their dreams. The city's vibrant colors and different forms of entertainment left me dazzled[21]. When I finally reached my hotel room, all of my energy instantly drained away and I slept soundly on my pillow. Perhaps this is the only way to escape from the bustling[22] streets of Las Vegas and enjoy the unrecognized side of its tranquility...

My first trip to the United States broadened[23] my vision and I felt strongly attracted to the country's modern appearance, its beauty and luxury, its extrovert[24] nature and its vivacity[25], which also consequently made me believe that it will become the land where I will pursue[26] my future dreams…

---

1 Spacious adj. 宽敞的:The hotel room was spacious and comfortable.

2 Fastened v. 系；上紧:Before taking off, the flight attendants checked if everyone on the plane had fastened their seatbelts.

3 Comprehend v. 了解到，领悟到:The meaning was difficult to comprehend.

4 Gripping adj. 扣人心弦的:The book had a gripping plot which made it hard for its readers to put it down.

5 Three-dimensional adj. 三维的:The new "Ice Age" is a three-dimensional movie.

6 Awe n. 惊奇:The place overwhelmed her with awe.

7 Spiraling v. 盘旋:The bus spiraled up the small mountain.

8 Sophistication n. 有学问，有内容的:Cufflinks add sophisitication to your attire.

9 Grandeur n. 壮观:Many tourists climb up the highest peak in order to get a chance to admire the grandeur of the mountain scenery.

10 (Be) Enamored (of /with /by) v. 迷恋;热爱;醉心于:It is quite obvious that he is enamored of Bella.

11 Imprint n. 印象:His ideas have left an imprint on people's minds.

12 Smalti n. 马赛克玻璃:The floor was covered with gorgeous smalti tiles.

13 Fused v. 合并;熔合:The material was fused with silver.

14 Internal adj. 内里的,内在的:A story's characters may experience both external and internal conflicts.

15 Glistening v. (进行时)闪烁:His eyes were glistening with tears.

16 Marvel n. 使人惊叹的人物或东西:James exclaimed: "The view at this height is a marvel!"

17 Initiative n. 最初的想法:They carried out their initiative to build a health center in rural Ecuador.

18 Breathtaking adj. 使人吃惊的,惊奇的:The large structure was simply breathtaking.

19 Flamboyant adj. 绚丽,艳丽:He likes to wear flamboyant clothing.

20 Energetic adj. 有活力的,有力气的:My neighbor's dog is very energetic.

21 Dazzled v. 使眼花:Lily was dazzled by the bright lights.

22 Bustling adj. 喧闹:Development in tourism has turned this once quiet and undiscovered area into a bustling little town.

23 Broadened v. (过去时)使扩大或加宽:Her interests broadened as she grew up.

24 Extrovert adj. 外向的:Her extrovert nature always seems to overcome awkward moments.

25 Vivacity n. 活泼:Julia's vivacity never failed to brighten people's day.

26 Pursue v. 追求:He is still unsure about what career he should pursue.

西安碑林游记

(初二)

西安是世界闻名的漫溢着古代文化韵味的城市：举世闻名的兵马俑、杨贵妃沐浴的华清池、华美富丽的大唐歌舞、风情百端的饺子宴。给我印象最深的是名人笔迹的作息之处——碑林。

跨过入口处的红色的门槛，我们来到了碑林。一眼看去是如此朴素，只是一个简单装潢的庭院被一些古桑树、矮草丛和杂花护着。闻着一股扑鼻的清香，我走进了一个高亭子，四根柱子支撑着，左右对称，刷着暗淡的红。里面耸立着一座碑，静静的，但却有一种无法形容的气势，如一本天降的圣书，令人不由心生敬畏。石碑上刻着密而整齐的字，右侧是方正的中文繁体，而左侧是曲直曼妙的蒙语。是一本中华圣经？是一章古典序言？我仔细阅读碑上的字，视线所及，多次读到"孝"字，可见中国人对此的重视，真可谓"百善孝为先"。我不自觉地用双手触摸那石碑，感到一阵冰凉，随之，整个身体颤了一下，它似乎像一个时光穿梭机，使我眼前浮现了古往今来的文人墨客挥笔成章、阅书万卷、乐在其中的生动画面。

沿着石路，又跨过一道门槛，来到一间展厅。那些古老的石碑被一个个玻璃罩保护着，一道道细碎的裂纹爬上了碑面，为之增添了些许沧桑，但却依然坚挺直立、气宇轩昂。古碑之神圣，风格之俊朗，内涵之丰富，历史之久远，使我肃然。

一阵鲜墨的香气引我进入了又一个展厅。只见一位中年男子熟练地往宣纸上刷墨，拓下千古文字。随着拍刷的节奏，一张张拓纸叠成厚厚的书本，似千张智者的嘴，娓娓倾吐着百年前的文明密码。"啪啪，啪啪……"回响在古城墙内外，期盼着现代文明的回应。

THE STELE FOREST, XI'AN

(Grade 8)

Xi An is a city well-known for its strong cultural atmosphere; it has the famous Terracotta warriors, Yang Guifei's bathing pool—Hua Qing Chi, extravagant[①] Tang Dynasty performances and exquisite[②] dumpling feasts. Yet, what left the greatest impression on me was where the writings of famous calligraphers[③] remain—the Stele[④] Forest.

Stepping over the high red doorsill at the entrance, I entered the Stele Forest. The place attracted me with its simplicity: it was austerely[⑤] constructed with only a small courtyard that was surrounded by old mulberry[⑥] trees, patches of green grass and flowers. While breathing the smell of fresh cut grass, I came to a tall symmetrical[⑦] pavilion[⑧], which was supported by four upright columns[⑨] painted in a faded color of deep red. Inside it stood a stele, in quietude[⑩], but in an imposing[⑪] manner, like a sacred[⑫] book from heaven, arousing[⑬] my reverence[⑭] towards its existence. Neatly carved characters covered the stele on the right side in squared, disciplined[⑮] traditional Chinese and the left side in the more abstract, cursive

Mongolian. Is it a Scripture[16]? Is it an ancient preface? I took a step closer to carefully observe the writings on the stele, and at a certain height, I found numerous appearances of the Chinese character "孝"(xiào), illustrating the importance of the "filial piety[17]", taught in Confucian Ideals, to the Chinese people. On an impulse, I touched the stele, and was greeted by a layer of icy cold that surged[18] up from the tip of my fingers like a wave of electricity and caused me to shiver. The delicate carvings inscribed on the stele, as if they were a time machine, caused images of the activities of ancient scholars to appear across my mind...

Following a stone paved road, I stepped over another doorsill and found myself in a display room. There, the oldest steles rested inside individual glass covers, with cracks that had gradually crawled over their surfaces, but they still stood erect[19], exuding[20] dignity[21]. Through the glass, I could feel a sacrosanctity[22], and profuse[23] wisdom and age, which aroused my respect.

I caught a whiff of fresh Chinese ink that lead me to another display room nearby. A middle-aged man was swiftly brushing even layers of ink on the stele and later printed its inscriptions onto sheets of rice paper. Following the consistent beat of brushing and dabbing[24], sheets of rice paper piled up into a thick stack and were bound into books that seemed to whisper the secret code of China's ancient culture. "Pat-pat, pat-pat" ⋯ the sound of the printing process echoed against the surrounding walls, as if it was waiting for the present to respond.

> 1 Extravagant adj. 奢侈的, 奢华的:The hall was filled with extravagant paintings.
> 2 Exquisite adj. 精致的:The restaurant served the most exquisite delicacies.
> 3 Calligraphers n. (复数)书法家:The original works of famous calligraphers are very expensive.
> 4 Stele n. 石碑:The stone stele has many ancient characters engraved on it.
> 5 Austerely adv. 简朴地,简单地:Although the exterior of the museum was austerely designed, it contained many valuable paintings from all over the world.
> 6 Mulberry n. 桑树:There are many mulberry trees in the park.
> 7 Symmetrical adj. 对称的:The images on the page are symmetrical.
> 8 Pavilion n. 亭子:The two tourists decided to take a rest inside the nearby pavilion.
> 9 Columns n. (复数)圆柱子:Three columns were used to support the roof.
> 10 Quietude n. 宁静,安静的状态:He sat in quietude.
> 11 Imposing adj. 壮丽, 壮大的:The imposing mansion stood on top of a hill near the sea.
> 12 Sacred adj. 神圣的:There is an impressive collection of sacred Hindu texts inside this temple.
> 13 Arousing v. (进行时)激发:The uneasiness given away by the man's facial expression arous [ed] (过去时) the police's suspicion.
> 14 Reverence n. 尊敬, 敬畏:The place inspired quiet reverence.
> 15 Disciplined adj. 有条理和规则的:The party members were all very disciplined and faithful to their leader.
> 16 Scripture n. 圣经:She made many references to the Scripture in her speech.

17 Filial piety n. 孝道: Filial piety is considered the first virtue in Chinese culture.

18 Surged v. (过去时)涌上: Fear surged within him as he heard approaching footsteps.

19 Erect adj. 直立的, 竖立的: The soldiers stood erect with their arms firmly by their sides.

20 Exuding v. (进行时)散发出: He exud [ed] (过去式) confidence in his job interview.

21 Dignity n. 尊严: Mr. Robinson is a respectable man of great dignity.

22 Sacrosanctity n. 神圣不可侵犯: The church possessed a sense of sacrosanctity.

23 Profuse adj. 丰富的: Her profuse vocabulary impressed the examiners.

24 Dabbing v. 轻轻地按或拍打: The girl dab [bed] (过去时) her mouth with her napkin.

山西常家大院游记

(初三)

农历新年我回到了父亲的家乡山西省太原市。这一天是正月初五,按传统的习俗,是送走财神的日子。清晨的爆竹声把我从睡梦中惊醒,新年热闹的一天又开始了。今天我和父母准备去参观慕名已久的山西晋商之府——常家大院。

常家大院原本有60万平方米,但因抗日战争时期日军的侵略及中国"文革"时期人为的破坏,目前能看到的仅是原来的五分之一,很让人惋惜。从外观上看,整个建筑由上而下呈阶梯样,形状规则,一色的青灰色砖瓦在黄土坡上显得格外气派。走进院内,我发现墙壁上常见的雕刻图案是瓶、鼎、琴棋书画、葡萄和梅花。听导游介绍,"瓶"的谐音为"平",代表着希望家人平平安安;"鼎"为君子守信的"一言九鼎";琴棋书画代表的是常氏家族成员必备的艺术技能;葡萄意味着果实累累,含义是传宗接代、子孙满堂;梅花则代表的是君子之花,期望的是家族成员都能具有君子风范。此外,还有很多有趣的砖雕,大多饱含着常氏家族希望祖业祖训能代代相传的愿望。如他们所愿,现在常氏家族的后代们居住在世界各地,几乎每年大家都会在农历正月初二这天回家团聚、祭祖。

走进大院的一处经典老宅,我看到了一座模仿历史名人的书法墙碑,绘有人物图案和历史纪录等。在那些模仿名人的书法中,除了惊叹它们充满神韵的笔迹,还让我体会到了"字如其人"的俗语,从模仿的字迹中,大致能看出被模仿者的性情。比如,一个临摹某位皇帝写的一个"静"字,形如舞蹈中的美女,可以猜测这也许是一位既爱江山又爱美人的君主。我边走边看,深切体会着这个有千年历史的山西大家族的家族文化和商业灵魂,真是受益匪浅。

参观完居室后,我们来到了一个很大的后花园,园内有一个形状优美的内湖和伫立在湖边的亭塔。整个花园给人的感觉是,既有南方园林的亭水交映、树鸟相依的秀丽,又有北方宫廷的山石奇异、松塔并立的大气。我和父亲登上了园中最高的观望塔,从塔峰一览常家大院的全景,心中顿生《登鹳雀楼》中的名句"欲穷千里目,更上一层楼"的感慨。

走下观望塔,发现塔后有一座安静的小庭院,庭院中央是一个多边形的水池。导游告诉我们,这水池是常氏家族的后生们读书写字时专用的洗墨池。仔细观察可以发现,那池壁上隐隐留下的墨迹,不禁又使我感受到了常氏家族的文化气韵。

游览结束后,当我沐浴着夕阳走出常家大院时,心中油然升起对晋商文化及常氏家族历史的由衷敬意。

THE CHANG FAMILY COURTYARD, SHANXI PROVINCE

(Grade 9)

During the Chinese New Year, I visited my father's hometown, Taiyuan city, in Shanxi province. According to Chinese tradition, the fifth day of the first month is when people send away the Chinese god of wealth. On that day, high-spirited① firecrackers once again woke me up in the early morning, which was a sign that another day of celebration had begun. My parents and I decided to go to a famous courtyard belonging to one of the Shanxi traders' families—the Courtyard of Chang's Family.

Chang's Courtyard originally covered an area of six hundred thousand square meters, but unfortunately, due to the invasion② during the Sino-Japanese War and the damage caused during the Chinese Revolution, it is now only one-fifth of its initial③ size. From its exterior, we could see that the structure slopes up in the style of a stairway, built from solid grey bricks, which seemed to emphasize its majestic④ quality. As I walked inside the courtyard, I observed that the carved images on the walls were mostly vases, tripods⑤, Chinese lutes⑥, chess, books, paintings, grapes and plum blossoms[7]. Our guide told us that "瓶" (ping: the vases) have the same pronunciation as the "平" in "平安" (píng ān: safe and sound), which displays the hope for every family member to be well; "鼎"(dǐng: the tripods) represents "一言九鼎" (yī yán jiǔ dǐng), which means to be trustworthy[8], a quality sought in a man of moral integrity[9]; the Chinese lutes, chess, books and paintings show the essential artistic talents that everyone in the Chang family must possess[10]; the grapes mean "fruitful[11]", which symbolizes[12] the continuation of the ancestral[13] line; and the plum blossom is the flower of integrity, implying the family's expectation[14] for their younger generation to become upright and responsible individuals. There are also many other interesting figures carved on the wall, and most of them convey the message of the family's hope to continue the family tree. And just as they had wished, descendents[15] of the Chang family still live in different places around the world, and visit the old courtyard on the second day of the first month of nearly every year.

Entering one of the dwellings[16] in the courtyard, I saw a wall that exhibited many stone tablets inscribed with imitations of works of famous calligraphers; drawings of people and historical records of the family. Looking at the inscriptions[17], apart from being impressed by the handsome penmanship[18], I acknowledged the old saying of "the person's handwriting is like the person himself" as I understood the art of inferring[19] the original writers' disposition[20] from their calligraphy. For example, from noting the shape and style of an imitation of the word "静"(jing: tranquility) written by a Chinese emperor, I could see it looked like a beautiful dancing lady, and thus I could guess that he may have been a ruler who loved his country as well as charming ladies. As I walked and observed my surroundings, I strongly felt the inspiring customs[21] and the respectable business spirit of this big Shanxi family with a history of over a thousand years.

After visiting one of the bedrooms, we came to a large backyard. Inside, there was a beautifully shaped pond and a small pavilion that stood beside it. The garden gave me the impression of an exquisite combination: the subtle picture of ponds reflecting the image of pavilions from its surface; birds chirping in a lively way on trees seen in southern China, and the sight of decorative stones, pines and temples found in the majestic palaces in northern China. My father and I went up the highest observation tower in the courtyard and viewed the entire courtyard from above, which allowed me to comprehend the famous line of the poem Deng Guan Que Lou: "if you wish to enjoy a greater sight, you must climb to a greater height."

Coming down from the tower, I realized that another garden was located quietly behind it, and its center was a pond with an irregular[22] shape. The guide told us that the pond was used to clean the brushes that the younger generation of the family used when they studied or wrote on other occasions. From carefully observing the sides of the pond, I saw ink stains that still faintly remained on the rocks, which made me feel and appreciate the Chang family's erudition[23].

After the tour, as I walked out of the courtyard at sunset, I felt a sudden respect towards the traders of Shanxi that the Chang family's long history roused[24] within me.

---

1 High-spirited   adj. 欢快的:The mall was filled with high-spirited Christmas shoppers.

2 Invasion   n. 侵略:The town was unable to defend itself from invasion.

3 Initial adj. 最初的:Changes were made to their initial plan.

4 Majestic   adj. 大气的,庄严的:The shadow of a majestic hawk loomed over me.

5 Tripods   n.   鼎:Bronze tripods are commonly seen in Chinese temples.

6 Chinese lutes   n.   中式古琴:The woman played a beautiful song on her Chinese lute.

7 Plum blossoms   n.   梅花:Plum blossoms flower in winter.

8 Trustworthy   adj.   值得信任的:Jim is one of Lenny's most diligent and trustworthy colleagues.

9 Integrity   n.   正直,诚实:Proctor is a man of great integrity.

10 Possess   v.   拥有,必备:She does not possess a great sense of humor.

11 Fruitful adj. 果实累累:The apple tree in our garden is very fruitful this year.

12 Symbolizes   v.   代表:The image of a crown symbolizes strength and royalty.

13 Ancestral   adj. 祖先的:The family pays a visit to their

ancestral home once every two years.

14 Expectation n. 期望:Her mother has high expectations for her future.

15 Descendents n. 后代:The descendents of the Wu family still live in Gui Zhou.

16 Dwelling n. 住宅:He always invites guests to his dwelling.

17 Inscriptions n. 碑文:The archeologist carefully examined the inscriptions on the tablet.

18 Penmanship n. 书法,笔迹:The children practiced their penmanship every Wednesday.

19 Inferring v. 猜测,臆测:From these facts we can infer that Rachel is innocent.

20 Disposition n. 性情;性质:Lily has a placid disposition.

21 Customs n. 传统:Eating dumplings on Chinese New Years Eve is a traditional Chinese custom.

22 Irregular adj. 不规则的:The bottle has an irregular shape.

23 Erudition n. 博学;学识;学问:Her speech reflects her erudition.

24 Roused adj. 激发(感情):His evasiveness roused her curiousity.

西班牙游记

（高一）

高一下半学期，正值繁花盛开的4月，学校组织西语班的学生去西班牙学习旅游。因我也略知一些西班牙语，便随团来到了西班牙的马德里。

上完两天有趣的西语课，第三天下午，我们沐浴着阳光，走进了马德里的露天斗牛场。斗牛是西班牙文化的主要组成部分，以往我只在电视上看到过一些场面的片断，感觉那是一种紧张、刺激的观赏项目。而那天，我们坐在铺着皮垫的石凳阶上，等待现场表演的开始。

表演即将开始，全场的观众为了悼念一位刚刚去世的著名老斗牛士静默了一分钟。接着，在一个小小的仪式后，斗牛士们拿着一件两面分别为黄、粉两色的斗篷站在了木栏后面。

随着一头健壮的公牛的出场，斗牛士们快步上前，用斗篷的粉红色面迎接他们的挑战对象。他们小心而很有技巧地接近公牛，把斗篷在身侧抖了抖，向公牛宣战。当公牛被激怒向他们猛跑而去时，斗牛士们便急速而退，返回到木栏内侧。

经过几次激烈回合后,公牛渐渐显得疲惫,反应速度也慢了下来。这时长矛手骑着裹着护甲的马而来,把长矛快速、准确地扎入公牛背颈部,进行放血。随后,为了进一步消耗公牛的体力,3个花镖手又将几个带利钩的花镖瞬间再度刺进公牛的背部,此时赢来了全场的掌声与喝彩。

面对如此场面,我震惊不已,对公牛的同情使我没有兴致和大家一起鼓掌欢呼。

表演的最后阶段,手持利剑和红斗篷的斗牛士上场,展示了更高难度的对公牛的挑衅动作,把全场的气氛推向高潮。但出乎意料的是,受伤的公牛竟突然一跃而起,袭击了斗牛士,斗牛士的右腿部流出大量的血。我不禁用手蒙住眼睛,同来的低年级同学被吓得哭了起来。但几分钟后,斗牛士拐着被包扎的右腿,又重新回到了场上。

在观众们此起彼伏的欢呼声中,他把斗牛最后的刺杀完成得干净利落。公牛最终在坚持了几秒钟后,摔倒在地。最后死去的公牛被几匹马拖着,绕场一周,宣告第一场表演的结束。我敬佩斗牛士们的勇敢和坚强,但更同情那只,不,那群,以及所有的被刺死的公牛。当我走出斗牛场后,带着如此的心情低下头,默默地为那些死去的公牛们祈祷。

第四天,我们乘大巴前往西班牙的古城——美丽的拖莱多市,使我一扫观看斗牛表演后的伤感。小城坐落在马德里郊外的一座山上。远方的田园似乎与天相连,朵朵白云舒展地躺在浅蓝色的晴空中。近处,一群黑白色的牛正在慢慢地咀嚼着清晨鲜嫩的绿草,巴士的窗口定格了一幅幅自然的画面。大巴盘旋而上,行驶了10多分钟,停在山顶。放眼望去,全城的景色尽收眼底。透明的空气中,碧蓝而清澈的塔霍河环抱着这座经典的欧式古城,河道中一处玲珑的小瀑布,欢快地拍打出白色透明的水花。整个城市的色调虽不鲜艳,却古朴、淡雅。远处的古式钟楼和城堡清晰可见,透着浓厚的历史感。

下山后,我们走进这美丽的古城,街头处处可见各种精致新奇的小饰品店。听导游说,这里的艺术品很著名,不少本土有名的画家都在这里生活过,难怪小店中的饰品都很有艺术性,也许正是这种氛围造就了一批有才气的艺术家吧。

沿着艺术之路,我们来到了古城著名的拖莱多大教堂。教堂的建筑耗时200多年。穿过青灰色的外墙,走进教堂中央,我眼前顿时金碧辉煌:绚丽的金铁门上雕刻着耶稣十字架,门栏后面是绘制着精细的圣经故事的组塑,教堂顶端悬挂着耀眼的吊灯,而大部分顶部都是由透光的彩色玻璃组成的。教堂的每一处都是精雕细刻,富丽堂皇,可见拖莱多人对宗教的崇敬。

我来到教堂内的一间展厅,入口处的两侧排列着同样上着锁的木雕柜子。听管理员说,右边的柜子是左边的复制品,大约在公元前18世纪完成,两个柜子里面存放着关于教堂重要的文件和记录。我上前仔细浏览柜子上所雕刻的各种图案，众多的天使和动物们个个都栩栩如生，很值得品味。展厅的墙壁上挂着一两百幅教皇的画像，显示出教堂的悠久历史。每位教皇手中各自握着不同的手杖，表情庄严而肃静，让人颇为感叹。

  短短几天的西班牙之旅结束了，但有趣的西语学习，刺激又残忍的斗牛场面，美丽的拖莱多市和庄严高耸的大教堂却交替出现在我的脑海中。

  别了，让我喜爱又让我感伤的西班牙，我还会再来！

SPAIN

(Grade 10)

In the blooming month of April, during the second half term of grade ten, my school organized a study trip to Spain. Because I had studied Spanish before, I decided to follow the Spanish class students for an experience in the capital city of Madrid.

After two days of Spanish classes, on the third afternoon, we visited the bullfighting stadium in Madrid. Bullfighting has always been an essential[①] part of Spanish culture, and I have watched parts of it on television before, which had left me with the impression that it is a sport full of tension and excitement. But on that day, we had the chance to visit the actual arena; sitting on stone steps with our rented cushions, we waited for the performance to begin.

When the bullfighting performance was about to start, everyone in the stadium stood up for one minute of silence to commemorate[②] an old and respected bullfighter who had just passed away the day before. After a small ceremony, bullfighters entered the arena[③], holding their capes[④] in yellow on one side and pink on the other, to take their places behind separate wooden fences.

As one burly[5] bull was released into the stadium, bullfighters came up to it speedily and used the pink side of their capes to greet their challenger. They moved carefully and tactically[6] towards the bull and shook their capes at their sides, declaring battle. When the bull dashed[7] towards them, the bullfighters quickly backed behind their fences. After several rounds, the bull was fatigued[8] and reacted more slowly. This was when the picador[9] came in, riding on a horse that wore armor, and rapidly and accurately stabbed[10] the bull in the back of its neck, so it would lose blood. To further weaken the bull, the three banderilleros[11] each attempted[12] to wound the bull with razor[13] sharp barbed sticks on its neck, which action received loud cheers and applause from the audience.

Witnessing such a situation, I found myself in absolute shock, and my sympathy[14] towards the bull left me with no enthusiasm to cheer with the crowd.

During the last part of the performance, the main bullfighter finally appeared with his red cape and his sword and began to demonstrate[15] challenging movements that drew the bull as close to him as possible, showing his control over it, which pushed the performance to its climax[16]. All of a sudden, the bull leaped and attacked the bullfighter unexpectedly, which left his right leg bleeding. I instinctively covered my eyes with my hands, and some of the younger students in our group were frightened to tears. But to our surprise, a few minutes later, the bullfighter, dragging his injured right leg, reappeared[17] in the arena.

Surrounded by the cheering of the excited crowd, the bullfighter completed the final stage with a clean kill. After resisting for a few seconds, the bull eventually collapsed on the floor. The dead bull was then hooked to a few horses which dragged it around the arena for one round, announcing that the first performance had ended. I admire the courage and persistence of the bullfighters, but feel more sympathetic towards every single bull that had been victimized in these bullfighting events. As I walked out of the stadium, I lowered my head in compassion[18] and began to quietly pray for and contemplate[19] all of the bulls that had been killed in these vicious[20] battles…

On the fourth day, we rode a bus to a beautiful old Spanish city—Toledo, which helped to wipe away my misery after watching the bullfight. The city was settled on a small mountain beyond the outskirts[21] of Madrid. Afar[22], the grass plain seemed to merge[23] with the light blue sky with several white clouds stretching lazily above it; and nearby, a herd of black and white cows chewed in a leisurely[24] way on the dewy[25] morning grass, filling each bus window with picturesque[26] images of nature. Reaching a mountain, the bus spiraled up, drove for another twenty minutes and stopped at the peak. As we jumped off the bus and looked out, the whole city presented itself in front of our eyes:

surrounded by fresh clean air, the clear blue Tagus river embraced[27] the old town with a small waterfall splashing white splatters within its course. Although the city was not brightly colored, its subtle[28] tone of brick red and grey gave it a quality of refined[29] elegance. The old clock tower and buildings stood charmingly in the distance, exuding a strong aura[30] of age and history.

As we came back to the foot of the mountain, we walked into this beautiful old town and saw that little souvenir and antique shops mainly occupied its streets. Our tour guide told us that the city is well known for its art works and many renowned Spanish artists had lived here; no wonder every object displayed in the shop window looked very artistic. I suppose that this atmosphere was what it took to create a group of talented artists.

Traveling along the "path of art", we arrived at the famous Toledo Cathedral. It took approximately two hundred years to construct this marvel. As I passed through its grey walls and came to the middle of the cathedral, I found myself surrounded by a sight rich with spectacular gold: an elaborate[31] golden gate had the crucifix[32] carved above it and a magnificent altarpiece[33], illustrating[34] the New Testament in remarkable[35] detail, towering[36] behind it; from the church ceiling hung a brilliant chandelier[37] and stained glass windows formed most of the upper walls. Every corner of the cathedral was filled with intricate[38] detail and magisterial beauty, reflecting the people of Toledo's great reverence towards their religion.

I walked towards a display room inside the cathedral and was greeted by two identical locked cupboards at the two sides of the entranceway. The watchman told us that the right cupboard was an eighteenth-century copy of the one on the left and both of the cupboards are used to store important documents and records of the cathedral. I moved closer and observed the fine carvings of lifelike[39] angels and animals, and was reluctant[40] to take my eyes off from them. The walls of the display room were lined with one or two hundred portraits of different Popes[41], illustrating the long history of the cathedral. Every Pope held a Papal Cross[42] and wore a dignified and solemn[43] expression, which earned people's thoughtfulness and respect.

My few days in Spain finally came to an end, but moments during the enjoyable Spanish classes, the exciting yet brutal[44] bullfighting and the visit to Toledo's renowned and colossal[45] cathedral keep recurring in my mind.

Farewell Spain, a country which I adore yet which also evoked[46] my sentimentality[47]. I will return someday…

---

1 Essential adj. 主要的，紧要的：It is essential to review your notes carefully for the test.

2 Commemorate v. 悼念，纪念：A ceremony was held at the town hall to commemorate those who had died in the war.

3 Arena n. 竞争场所：The crowd cheered as the athletes entered the arena.

4 Capes n. 斗篷：She wore her cape the wrong way.

5 Burly adj. 健壮的：The burly wrestler intimidated the

young child.

6 Tactically adv. 策略高明地;机智、熟练地:He retreated tactically.

7 Dashed v. 冲:The rabbit dashed into the bushes at the sight of me.

8 Fatigued v. 疲乏,劳累:The family was fatigued by their long journey.

9 Picador n. 长矛手:The picador speared the bull with a lance.

10 Stabbed v. 刺入,刺伤:He was stabbed in the leg.

11 Banderilleros n. (西班牙语)花镖手:The three banderilleros entered the arena after the picador had injured the bull.

12 Attempted v. 试图:He attempted to persuade his mother to allow him to go on the trip.

13 Razor n. 刮刀:The little boy accidently cut himself with his father's razor.

14 Sympathy n. 同情的情感:She had great sympathy for the families that had lost their children during the war.

15 Demonstrate v. 演示,表演:The zookeeper demonstrated how to hold a snake.

16 Climax n. 最高潮:The climax of the story was when the hungry bear caught up with the man.

17 Reappeared v. (过去时)重现:Her husband reappeared after having left her years ago.

18 Compassion n. 怜悯,同情:The victims should be sheltered and treated with compassion.

19 Contemplate v. 熟思,沉思:The holocaust is too horrifying to contemplate.

20 Vicious adj. 残忍的,凶恶的:The vicious assault caused many innocent deaths in the village.

21 Outskirts n. 郊外:Urban development is increasing its pace in the outskirts of Beijing.

22 Afar adj. 远处:The vase looked flawless from afar.

23 Merge v. 合并,融会:He merged into the darkness.

24 Leisurely adv. 轻松地,放松地:The old man walked leisurely in the park.

25 Dewy adj. 被露水滋润的:The photographer took many close-up shots of the dewy grass.

26 Picturesque adj. 如画的:Sally was mesmerized by the picturesque view outside her hotel window.

27 Embraced v. (过去时)拥抱;环抱:Helen's grandmother embraced her warmly when she arrived at the airport.

28 Subtle adj. 暗淡的,不起眼的:The subtle colors in the room seemed to have a soothing effect.

29 Refined adj. 精致的；优雅的:Ten years of living and studying abroad have shaped her into a refined lady.

30 Aura n. 气质:The place retains an aura of sophistication.

31 Elaborate adj. 精细的,精巧的:The tourists admired the elaborate carvings on the wall.

32 Crucifix n. 十字架:The crucifix is found in every church.

33 Altarpiece n. 组塑:The altarpiece was painted by a famous Italian artist.

34 Illustrating v. (进行时)绘制:The scroll illustrat[es](第三人称现在时)the original appearance of the palace before it was damaged.

35 Remarkable adj. 值得注意的，惊人的:He has won remarkable success.

36 Towering v. (进行时) 耸立:The shadow of the monster tower[ed](过去时)over him.

37 Chandelier n. 吊灯:There is a chandelier in the ballroom.

38 Intricate adj. 细微的,精致的:This piece of art is full of intricate details.

39 Lifelike adj. 逼真的,栩栩如生的:The bird painted on canvas was so lifelike that it seemed like it would fly out of the frame at any moment.

40 Reluctant adj. 不情愿的:She was reluctant to take his orders.

41 Popes n. (复数) 教皇:The Pope paid a visit to the U.S.

42 Papal Cross n. 教皇的手杖:The Pope held his Papal Cross as he gave his blessing.

43 Solemn adj. 庄严的,严肃的:The queen wore a solemn expression.

44 Brutal adj. 暴力的:The prisoners received brutal punishments.

45 Colossal adj. 巨大的,高大的:The colossal tower dominated the view of the town.

46 Evoked v. 唤起;引起:The strong images conveyed in the poem evoked memories of her childhood.

47 Sentimentality n. 感伤:His plays often verge on sentimentality.

III.
THOUGHTS AND INSPIRATIONS...
思考和感悟

2008 年 AUTUMN, IN BEIJING, CHINA
二〇〇八年 秋，中国北京

老 人

这首诗是2009年在跟着德威合唱团来到香港的一家老人院后,在与老年人的接触和交流中有感而发后所写的。

岁月静静地叠落在他们的脸颊,
微笑时显露出深深的刻痕。
他们举起那双颤抖的手,
试图够摸那双稚嫩的芽,
紧紧地握住。
一瞬间,
双眼泛出泪水的光。

他们虚弱的身躯后,
是儿时、成年时、壮年时,
那永远说不完的故事,
讲不完的话。

而那份内心顽强的生命力,
令年轻的我们用崇敬的目光凝视着他。

他们经历过战争与和平、欢乐和苦难;
他们见证过世界许多地方,
而这一切又等待我们去学习、闯荡。
他们曾经和我们一样探索着世界,
用青春、热情和力量,
但那些对往事的记忆,
对他们也许不再久长。

此时他们正微笑地看着我们,
似乎从岁月的镜头中,
又看见了几十年前的自像。
他们回想着、追忆着,
轻拍着我们的背,颤摇着他们的头。
或许在叹息光阴竟如此之快地从他们的指缝中悄然滑过,
如烟云过往……

The Elderly

This is a poem that I wrote after visiting a home for the elderly in Hong Kong during the 2009 Dulwich Chamber Choir Trip in February.

Age, crawling on their faces and
leaving traces of lines that deepen as they smile.
Their shaky hands, reaching
out and then catching another hand of
youth, and grasping on tight,
which instantly makes their eyes
glisten[①].

Beneath their outward feebleness[②]
are everlasting[③] stories and remarks
of youth, adolescence[④], adulthood,
and inconceivable[⑤] strengths
that leave the young
staring back at them in admiration
and awe.

They have gone through peace and wars, joy and sorrow;

they have seen parts of the world we've still yet to learn,

but they were once like us—

young, strong, experimenting with the

world, and fascinated

by things they may no longer be able to

recall.

But now they look at us and smile,

as if we mirror themselves some fifty years ago.

They reflect and reminisce⑥,

then pat us on the back, shaking their

heads, as they realize how

time has effortlessly⑦ slipped through their hands

so fast.

---

1 Glisten v. 闪烁,发光:Her cheeks glisten [ed] （过去时）with tears.

2 Feebleness n.虚弱;微弱:His increasing feebleness made his son worry.

3 Everlasting adj. 永久的;永恒的:This experience left her with everlasting memories.

4 Adolescence n. 青春期:Children often become rebellious when they are going through adolescence.

5 Inconceivable adj. 无法想象的；不可思议的:They treated their hostages with inconceivable brutality.

6 Reminisce v. 回味, 回想:The old couple reminisced

about their first honeymoon in Bali.

7 Effortlessly adv. 丝毫不费力气地:The man picked up the heavy box effortlessly.

海的布鲁斯旋律

夜,
我听到大海在轻轻地放歌,
唱着那首快被遗忘的,
扣人心弦的布鲁斯。

在那优美的旋律中,
却隐含着凄凉与忧伤。
我的心被刺痛,
我的身在颤抖。

风,
跟着旋律轻轻拂动,
仿佛为大海凄美的歌伴奏。

瞬时间,
我仿佛窒息了,
那一个个音符顺着咽喉流入,

把我唤醒,

把我吞没。

我听清了,

听清了海的诉说,

曾经的碧蓝色变得混浊,

曾经的海植物渐渐稀少,

曾经的鱼群远走他处。

我感受到了,

感受到那是一种绝望的呐喊,

那是一种来自海底的哭唤。

它追溯着被时光遗失的梦,

它发泄着被世间抛弃的怒,

它倾吐着被人类不珍惜的痛。

它更要唤醒那份爱,

那份渐渐要被忘却,

那份被埋葬在一块块被开发,

被建筑的土地深处的爱!

Ocean Blues①

At night I heard the ocean gently sing,
humming the isolated② tune
of a heart-rending③ blues.

It was soft and tenderly sweet,
but with grieving④ notes of pain and sadness
that made me sting and shiver
with guilt I failed to define.

The wind stirred,
as it played along with whooshing sounds
that mingled⑤ with the sorrowful sea.

I gasped,
and the music trickled down my throat,
drowning,
overwhelming me.

I heard it;

那坠入深渊的恐惧，
却时刻在威胁。

更多的人则以智慧和正义，
挣脱了邪恶的缰绳，
赢得了真善之美，
成为了搏斗中的英雄。

在历史的脉管中，
从未停止过向前奔涌的血流。
蕴藏着善恶的血液里，
善，永远被多数人接受、赞扬。
也许，这就是历史更新、换代的动能！

HISTORY

This poem was inspired by my learning experience in history class. It contains my thoughts towards the true essence of the subject; and is focused on the aspect of good and evil throughout the course of history.

There are words of good and evil kept in quiet mouths,
    there are records of truth buried below the dirt
    and there are burnt or lost secrets in letters,
    but however concealed they may be,
    they still linger in memories of the remote[①] past.

Some are revealed,
for a few quiet mouths utter
when trust is found,
or when it's bewitched[②] by an intolerable[③] spell;
Some are unearthed[④],
for a few truths below our feet lure us
with enchanting whispers

I heard the ocean recounting⁶ its worries,

as its aquamarine⑦ color has been eaten away by the disposal⑧ of debris⑨,

as its wealthy resource of aquatic plants has shrunk and declined,

as its lively clusters of inhabitants have migrated further away.

I felt it;
I felt the unfathomable⑩ despair,
while the deep yelled out
and traced its unwanted dreams
from the submarine⑪,
and expressed its anger to be forgotten,
its agony⑫ to be taken for granted.
But most of all,
it was a call for the love
that is buried beneath our bloated⑬
and exploited⑭ land

Above.

> 1 Blues n.(音乐)布鲁斯:He sang the blues with his soul.
> 2 Isolated adj. 偏僻的:He lives in an isolated village that is two hours away from here by car.
> 3 Heart-rending adj. 使人感到悲伤的;凄凉的:The old lady was touched by his heart-rending story.
> 4 Grieving v. (进行时)使痛心:The process of grieving the loss of a loved one takes time.

5 Mingled v.(过去时)使混合;加入:The sound of the bells mingled with the lively chirping of the birds.

6 Recounting v. (进行时):Julia recount [ed] (过去时) the event to Bethy.

7 Aquamarine adj. 碧蓝的:The aquamarine lake glittered under the summer sun.

8 Disposal n. 处理;排除:The disposal of waste from factories has caused great concern about the environment of the scenic town.

9 Debris n. 垃圾,废物:The park called for volunteers who were willing to help with cleaning up the debris in the ponds.

10 Unfathomable adj. 深不可测的:The unfathomable depths of the sea have lead to many human imaginings.

11 Submarine adj. 海底的(在诗里是作为名词来使用): There are many submarine eruptions due to the movement of the plates of the Earth.

12 Agony n. 挣扎的痛苦;苦恼:He struggled in agony.

13 Bloated adj. 傲慢的;趾高气扬的:The men in the photo were bloated industrial leaders during the eighteenth century.

14 Exploited adj. 利用……谋私利:The locals have exploited a large area of their land over the past few decades due to the developments of the village in tourism.

历 史

这首诗是我在学习历史课的过程中对历史的实质和真谛的思考与感悟,并以善与恶的视角表达出来。

含食着善与恶的沉默之口,
深埋入土的真实记录,
焚毁或被遗失的秘密信件。
无论它们如何的隐蔽,
却都存活于时代的记忆。

它们被告之,
因为沉默之口打破了宁静,
或许是找到了信任,
或许是被无法抗拒之声所迷惑;
它们被挖掘,
因为被埋藏在土地下真相的涌动;
它们被拼凑成图,

因为那些在焚毁后留下的碎片；
它们被发现，
因为上个世纪被遗失的，
可能在这个世纪出现。

在这个过程中，
我们唤醒了，
唤醒了那些该或不该被唤醒的善与恶。

在时代的交替中，
善恶之界有时会在人们的视线中变得模糊，
它不如天地般清晰，
它不如黑白色易辨。

人们时刻在善恶间甄别，
一些人被恶的黑影笼罩；
被恶的冰冷冻结；
被恶的伪装欺骗，
进而被它吞食、击败。

一些人用生命与汗水，
搏击在善恶的悬崖，

那坠入深渊的恐惧,

却时刻在威胁。

更多的人则以智慧和正义,

挣脱了邪恶的缰绳,

赢得了真善之美,

成为了搏斗中的英雄。

在历史的脉管中,

从未停止过向前奔涌的血流。

蕴藏着善恶的血液里,

善,永远被多数人接受、赞扬。

也许,这就是历史更新、换代的动能!

HISTORY

This poem was inspired by my learning experience in history class. It contains my thoughts towards the true essence of the subject; and is focused on the aspect of good and evil throughout the course of history.

There are words of good and evil kept in quiet mouths,
    there are records of truth buried below the dirt
    and there are burnt or lost secrets in letters,
    but however concealed they may be,
    they still linger in memories of the remote[①] past.

Some are revealed,
for a few quiet mouths utter
when trust is found,
or when it's bewitched[②] by an intolerable[③] spell;
Some are unearthed[④],
for a few truths below our feet lure us
with enchanting whispers

to reach out for our shovel;
Some are deciphered[5],
for few of the written remains
are comprehensible when pieced together;
and some are discovered,
for those thought to be lost a century ago
can be found,
a century later.

During these findings,
we may rekindle[6],
rekindle the good and evil that should or should not awake.

But during the evolution of mankind,
the borders that separate the virtuous[7] and sinful[8] men

can sometimes become confusing to the eye.
It is not the same as the clear distinction of sky and earth,
nor is it the same as the blatant[9] difference between black and white.

We ponder between the two at every instant,
and some become overwhelmed by evil's looming[10] black figure;
frozen by its cold-blooded touch;

misled by its luring⑪ masquerade⑫,
and are then diminished, and vanquished⑬.

Others, mixed in sweat,
fight with their soul
on the cliff of good and evil,
while constantly feeling the threatening fear
of falling off the steep ledge⑭.

And the larger portion who remain,
struggle themselves free from the rope of evil
with their good judgment and integrity⑮,
winning the reward of rectitude⑯,
the name of hero.

The vessels of history
have never stopped powerful gushes of blood
containing constituents⑰ of both good and evil.
Yet righteousness has always been celebrated.
And this verity, perhaps,
is what reinvigorates⑱ history and its people throughout
its ceaseless⑲ course...

---

1 Remote adj. 很久以前的:Until this century, China's remote past was mainly known for its ancient culture.

2 Bewitched v. (过去时) 迷惑, 蛊惑:Everyone in the village believed that she was bewitched by a witch's spell.

3 Intolerable adj. 难以忍受或抵抗的:Johnny was fed up with the intolerable pressures of his work, so he quit.

4 Unearthed v. （过去时)(从地中) 挖掘:The excavators unearthed many fragments of pottery from an unknown era.

5 Deciphered v. （过去时）辨认，辨读:She could not decipher the code on the letter.

6 Rekindle v. 重新激起:Carla tried to rekindle her friendship with Rachel.

7 Virtuous adj. 有品德的，有道德的:People in the community consider Ms. Brown to be a virtuous lady because she is one of the few women who never get involved in neighborhood gossip.

8 Sinful adj. 有罪的；不道德的，邪恶的:He could not forgive his sinful past.

9 Blatant adj. 非常明显的:There was a blatant difference between the qualities of the two products.

10 Looming v. （进行时）如巨大的影子般出现:The looming clouds stretched across the village sky.

11 Luring v. 诱惑人的,吸引人的:The special offer lur[ed] (过去时) many customers to buy the product.

12 Masquerade n. 伪装,掩饰:His masquerade ended when he was arrested.

13 (Be) Vanquished v. 被征服,被打败:The country's opponents were vanquished.

14 Ledge n. 峭壁:A tall fence was installed to stop people from going near the ledge.

15 Integrity n. 气节:She is respected for her moral integrity.

16 Rectitude n. 正直:He is a model of rectitude.

17 Constituents n.(复数) 组成部分，成分:Individual constituents may affect the success of a solution.

18 Reinvigorates v. 使恢复生气，使重新振作:The new mayor introduced many projects that he believed would help reinvigorate the town's economy.

19 Ceaseless adj. 不停的:She is a ceaseless worker who strives for perfection.

黄色的大鸟

在英文课堂上学习美国阿瑟·米勒的著作——话剧《萨勒姆的女巫》(原名：《炼狱》)——的第三幕后,我对身为仆人的玛莉·华伦感触颇深。这篇诗文将我对这个人物的理解及心理活动的体验,以第一人称的形式,描述和再现了这个角色的情感表现及心理过程。

[背景介绍]

《萨勒姆的女巫》是美国作家阿瑟·米勒写于1953年的作品。作品的深意有着浓厚的政治色彩。他用谎言与真相来影射发生在1950年初的全美反共运动。剧中的女孩艾比盖尔·威廉姆斯因向剧中主人公约翰·普罗克托求爱被拒,则用复仇的方式公然在法庭上编造谎言来陷害他的妻子伊丽莎白·普罗克托。最初答应在法庭上揭示出真相的女仆玛莉·华伦却最终因经受不住艾比盖尔的谎言"轰炸",在经历了一番内心痛苦的挣扎后,为保全自己濒临崩溃的精神世界,违心地放弃了说出真相的初衷。屈服于谎言的她也站到了艾比盖尔的阵营,使普罗克托和他的家人继续担负着被谎言指控的罪名。

作者通过对上述人物的刻画,让人们意识到真相是可以被虚伪掩盖的,冤案是能在人为的谎言中形成的,从而启迪人们去思索和强化对事物的辨别能力及正义感。

她①惨叫着,
依然是那熟悉的并让我②感到心寒的声音。
这声音,从她那冲着空荡的天花板的咽喉里发出。

"你不能的！走开！我说走开！"
她貌似惊恐地指着那虚无的"黄鸟"吼叫着。
她身后的几个同伙们,
也配合着,望着她手指的方向。

"它在横梁上！在椽子后面！"
她的一个同伙也忍不住地起着哄。
她们都在玩这个谎言的游戏,
不禁撕心裂肺地尖叫着。

"为什么？"她似乎哽咽了,
稍停片刻,
她显得略微踌躇,
颤动着嘴唇,

"黄色的大鸟,你为什么来?"

她以无辜的神情继续着谎言,
把我的名字当成大鸟来叫。
她谎称我要将她的脸撕碎,
并暗示着周围我对她怀着一股邪恶的妒火。

我被震怒着,
"这一切都是假的、假的!"
我内心一遍遍重复着,
恳求着。
她的话语就如一条绳索,
勒紧了我的脖子。

我忍无可忍地哭喊着、吼叫着,
却被她们不停地重复、捉弄。
她们的声音把我一口一口吞没,
并使我的毅力渐渐地瓦解、崩溃。

一切都变得模糊,
我陷入了迷茫,
像是被摔成千万碎片,

感到如此的无助。

我看到她正盯着我,
从那眼神里,
我看到了极端和傲慢,
也看到了她那让我不寒而栗的兴奋。

我的血顿时变得冰凉,
我听到心脏急速的跳动声,
这声音刺痛着我,
在我体内形成巨大的回声。

所有的一切就如同一根麻绳,
紧紧地缠裹着我,
我浑身变得麻木,
像一个没了发条的电动玩具,
瘫倒在那里。

在这一刻,
我实在受不住了,
我放弃了对抗。
我要挣脱这一切获得自由。

我违心地把手指向了那个男人——

约翰·普罗克托③。

---

1 诗中的"她"是艾比盖尔·威廉姆斯,一个谎言的代表。

2 诗中的"我"是玛丽·华伦,一个由最初准备揭露谎言到最后屈服于谎言的女仆。

3 约翰·普罗克托,谎言的受害者,最希望揭穿谎言,还原真相的正义人物。

The Yellow Bird

While learning the third act of the well-known play, "The Crucible", written by American playwright Arthur Miller, I found myself greatly inspired by the timid maid, Mary Warren. This poem is my attempt at portraying my interpretation of her internal emotions in first person narration.

She[①] wails
   that familiar chilling, wild wail
   through the tube of her throat
   stretched towards the blank ceiling.

"You will not! Begone[②]! Begone, I say!"
she points with awe and fear,
followed by a subservient[③] militia[④]
gazing in her direction.

"It's on the beam! Behind the rafter!"
another cries upon an impulse.
They all knew how to play the game,

as their internal thrill squealed.

"Why-?" she gulps
a pause,
with a sudden hesitancy,
and whimpering⑤ lips.
"Why do you come, Yellow Bird?"

With her gulling⑥, convincing innocence,
she calls the bird my name
and claims I want to tear her face
goaded⑦ by odious⑧ envy.

I sprang.
"It is all pretence⑨, pretence!"
I repeated inside,
pleaded,
while she choked me alive
with her daunting⑩ words.

I shouted, I cried, I screamed.
All followed with their mesmerizing repetition
devouring⑪ me inch by inch
dissolving my determination.

It was all a blur
and I was stuck in vagueness,

feeling helpless, and shattered
into thousands of pieces.

Then I felt her look at me.
And from those eyes, I saw
her desperation, and vanity[12], and
ultimate exhilaration[13].

My blood ran cold
as I felt the quickening pulse from my bosom[14]
echoing in my cavity[15]
striking the walls piercingly[16].

Everything slithered[17] around me
like a rope, paralyzing[18] me,
like a wind-up toy that has lost its key.
I was overpowered.

It was then,
that I had to withdraw from the fight for justice
and release myself
with deceitful[19] blaming
by pointing my finger
at one man—

John Proctor[20].

1 "She" refers to Abigail Williams.

2 Begone （书面感叹句）走开！（表示极为厌烦）："Begone," the actor exclaimed.

3 Subservient adj. 充当手下或工具的：The little girl was subservient to her parents.

4 Militia n. 民兵；国民军：The militia fought bravely during the revolution.

5 Whimpering v. （进行时）呜咽着：She whimper[ed]（过去时）something inaudible.

6 Gulling v. （进行时）欺骗：Propaganda is used to gull（现在时）people into supporting the product or idea it advertises.

7 Goaded v. （过去时）激励，煽动：His actions were goaded by his ambition.

8 Odious adj. 极为可厌的：The dumpsite gave out an odious smell that could be smelt from hundreds of meters away.

9 Pretence n. 虚伪，假装：The company was unable to continue its pretense that everything was going well.

10 Daunting adj. 使人害怕的：She found an excuse to push away the daunting task that her boss asked her to carry out.

11 Devouring v. （进行时）吞没：The tiger devoured（过去时）its prey within minutes.

12 Vanity n. 虚荣：His vanity often irritated his co-workers.

13 Exhilaration n. 兴奋：She was exhilarated at the thought of going to Japan for Christmas.

14 Bosom n. 胸膛：She felt her heart wildly beat in her bosom.

15 Cavity n. 空腔：The human body consists of many different body cavities.

16 Piercingly adv. 如刺一般地：The high-pitched sound hit his eardrums piercingly.

17 Slithered v. （过去时）滑动；滑行：The snake slithered across the surface.

18 Paralyzing v. （进行时）使麻痹；使瘫痪：The old lady has been paralyzed（过去时）by a recent stroke.

19 Deceitful adj. 骗人的，不诚实的:His deceitful act fooled everyone in the community.

20 John Proctor 约翰·普罗克托： the main character of the play; a respectable man of integrity. He experiences a series of dilemmas throughout the course of the play, and finally chooses to preserve his name over his life.

Restavek 女孩儿

看完CNN国际新闻台的一个关于在海地的现代奴隶制度的报道,我十分震惊,无法想象奴隶制度竟仍存在于当今社会,因此决定以诗歌的形式表达我的感受和唤起人们对这里苦难的民众,特别是这些孩童们的注意。

诗里的女孩儿叫做Restavek,这个名字是起给那些因为家里太穷,被送到极恶劣的条件下做劳工的海地孩子们的。原本期望这样能够改进生活条件的家人们,却发现现实恰恰相反:这些孩子们不但得不到任何的收入,还要忍受主人的虐待和鞭打。

她面无表情地呆呆地看着地面,
用那极为虚弱的声音,
讲述着那些她必须干的活儿——
搓地板、倒夜壶、送水……
也倾听着她对爱的渴盼。

在她十四年的人生中,

竟从未得到过一个拥抱!

她抬起了头,

一双大大的眼睛充满了忧愁,

充满了彻骨的恐惧。

那眼神似乎预测到了下一次的鞭打,

看到了等待她的下一个苦役。

然而,她全部的酬劳却是

每晚给予她的几口剩饭。

我有了想把食物送入她口中的冲动,

我发自内心想给她那骨瘦如柴的身体

一个拥抱!

一种温暖!

一股力量!

想让她知道这个世界是有爱的,

想让她那消瘦的脸露出一丝的笑。

可惜我们相距得太远太远。

看她又在搓着地板,

拱着背半跪着,

露出一节节嶙峋的脊骨,

像一根根刺,

刺痛着我的双眼。

她倒完一家家的夜壶,

又去刷洗一摞摞碟碗,

还要准备去送那沉沉的五加仑[1]水。

五加仑的水每日七次倒满桶中,

当水满到要溢出桶时,

她便用那干枯如柴的手把桶顶在头上,

走上一条陡峭不平的小路,

摇晃的身影,

却再没有回头……

---

1 五加仑:(容积)约19升。

Restavek Girl

This poem was inspired by a news report on CNN about modern slavery in Haiti. I found it very shocking that the slave system is still present in our world, and so I decided to express my thoughts and raise awareness through the form of a poem.

The girl that I have written about in this poem is a Restavek, which is the name given to the poor families in Haiti that have sent their children out to work in terrible conditions with the hope of better standards of living. However, this is not the case, as these children are not paid and are treated with much brutality by their owners.

She stares at the ground, expressionless,
and murmuring in a voice
so weak, so brittle[①] that you can barely hear her words.
She speaks about work scrubbing the floor and
delivering water… and the lack
of love, as in her

fourteen years of life,
she had never been given a single hug.

She looks up, with large anxious eyes of
insecurity and fear
that seemed to anticipate another whipping or an
uncompromising② demand from her owner.
Yet, even having to endure③ such suffering,
she is only given scraps④ at the end of each grueling⑤
day.

How I wish to feed her and hold her
skeletal⑥ body, to give her
a hug,
some warmth,
and strength,
and to reassure her that there is love in the world
and help her put on a smile
on her dark face with those gaunt⑦ cheekbones
but we're so far apart.

She scrubs the floor, kneeling and bending
her back, with the bones of her spine
seen so sharply from behind,
like pricks⑧ under her skin
that pierce⑨ your eyes.
She empties the chamber pots⑩,

washes the dishes and then finally
goes to deliver five gallons of water.

Five gallons of water
are poured into a large bucket
to its brim⑪,
seven times a day, and she takes it,
using her bony arms and places it on her head.
As she cautiously balances it,
she walks up long steep rocky paths, shaking,
without looking back.

---

1 Brittle adj. 易碎的, 脆弱的: Due to malnutrition, the little girl's bones are very fragile and brittle.

2 Uncompromising adj. 毫无商量余地的: The uncompromising manager did not accept any excuses from his workers to be absent from work.

3 Endure v. 忍受: She was forced to endure whipping from her master.

4 Scraps n. 残羹剩饭: The beggar searched for edible scraps in the pile of trash.

5 Grueling adj. 使极度疲劳的: He was absolutely drained after his first grueling military practice.

6 Skeletal adj. 骨瘦如柴: The boy's skeletal body seemed so fragile that it looked like it would break at any moment.

7 Gaunt adj. 瘦削的: The man had a long gaunt face.

8 Pricks n. (复数)刺: The pin prick produced a drop of blood.

9 Pierce v. 刺入, 扎入: The thorn pierced her skin.

10 Chamber pots n. 尿壶, 夜壶: In some very undeveloped areas, people still use chamber pots at home.

11 Brim n. 边: Hot water was filled to the brim of the tub.

多元文化与我

我讲话,
却不会母语,
因我已忘却了我出生地的言语。

我站立,
却不知我归属于世界的何地,
因我祖籍和国籍各异。

我行走,
却不知最终会落脚在哪里,
因我继续在我走过的每一块土地、每一种文化中选择着……

我的旅程有着宽广的地域,
但却缺乏对地域了解的深度。
我在走过之处留下了一个个足印,

但浅浅的足印却难以渗入每块土地，

去触碰那支撑着地域核心的本土文化，

去深刻了解其文化的精髓，

很难把它们收入囊中，

继续前行。

旅程中，

我眼前的景色是多彩的，

但有时却让我困惑：

自问所在之处是否适合于我？

我的视角中，

富含着旅途中采集的各种元素，

它们的堆积把我推向高处，

不断开阔着我的视野。

同时它们又如同一条无形的绳索，

牵制着我，

使我视野的深度不免产生着局限。

旅途中，

我看到的世界千姿百态，

但它的轮廓却有时又显得粗糙和模糊。

还没等我停下，

透过"显微镜"让这一切透明、清晰,
又不得不匆匆上路,
继续前行。

视线中,
常会遇到来自民族各异、文化各异、信念各异的旅者们,
我们相处融洽。
但当我停留某处,与当地人交流相处,
偶尔会感到生疏与困惑。
我不断尝试着调整视角、态度及思维模式,
力求缩短其距离,
却感受到彻底掌握与接受某种传统文化,
是谈何容易!

这一切让我深深体验到:
我被来自旅程中的多元文化所影响,
所融合,
所塑造……
在无形中提升着我观察事物的能力,
却也增加了我彻底融入社会传统文化的难度。

这一切让我猛然醒悟到:

我的根，很难深埋在一个地域的土地之中，
更无法充分吸取其中的所有养分。

这一切也让我渐渐地意识到：
我观察着多元文化，
我感受着多元文化，
我倾听着多元文化，
我尝试着多元文化。
多元文化已注定成为我旅途中不可缺少的空气，
我将继续伴随着它呼吸、成长、前行……

在未来的人生旅途中，我会进一步思考和感悟多元文化对我的影响，尽力扩大和加强它的有益之处，缩小和弥补它的不足之处，在不断完善自我中前行。

MULTICULTURALISM[①] AND I

I speak,
not knowing what is my mother tongue,
as I have forgotten the language of my birthplace.

I stand,
not knowing where I belong,
as my heritage and nationality differ evidently[②].

I walk,
not knowing where I will finally settle down,
as I continue to deliberate on the different lands I have set foot on and cultures I have briefly learnt.

During the journey,
the walk is great in length,
but smaller in the depth of learning
of where I temporarily stand.
I have left footprints on various roads,
but not so steadily that they penetrate[③]

  into the core——the local traditions and history,
  to thoroughly understand the quintessence④ of each culture,
  and to pack them in my rucksack,
  Where they may cohere with or repel one another,
  as I move along.

  During my journey,
  the view is spectacular but
  it arouses my confusion, as I always question the place where I stand.
  The perspective that I have developed is alloyed⑤ with elements I have collected along this journey,
  and it seems to elevate me for a greater view, but at the same time,
  holds me back with the invisible strands of its variety,

  which limits concentration, and results in
  an inevitable circumscription⑥
  in my view.

  During my journey,
  I see the world, big and wide,
  as if it contains everything,
  but the outlines of its landscapes are rough and vague,
  lacking precision and detail.

I wish to sharpen my view by adjusting the lens of my microscope,
 but before I see the image clearly,
 I realize I must once again
 hit the road.

During my journey,
I meet people of
different races, cultures, beliefs,
 and find myself comfortably relating to international travelers, like me,
  but often feel a sense of disparity between the locals
   of the country of my heritage, my birthplace or where I have lived… and me.
 I try to minimize this difference by adjusting my views, attitude and thoughts,
  but figure that not all customs are easy to
  comprehend and grasp
  and accept.

All allow me to recognize:
 I have been influenced and shaped by multiculturalism—an amalgamation[7] from my journey,
  which enhances my vision towards society,
  and makes me become aware of its activities.

All allow me to comprehend:

my roots are not deeply sunk down into the ground,
or fully taking up and assimilating⑧ the nutrients
of a particular piece of land.

All allow me to perceive:
I see diversity, I feel diversity, I hear diversity, and I taste diversity.
It is the air I travel in,
use to respire⑨, and use to grow.

During the course of my journey in the future, I will continue to contemplate and consider the influences of multiculturalism on me, and make an effort to expand and develop its merit⑩ while minimizing and offsetting⑪ its defects⑫, to shape myself to become a better person.

1 Multiculturalism n. 多元文化:Some people promote multiculturalism, while others prefer to retain their own traditional culture.

2 Evidently adv. 明显地:The two ideas contradicted each other evidently.

3 Penetrate v. 渗入,贯穿:X-rays cannot penetrate through lead.

4 Quintessence n. 精华;精髓:The wine personified the quintessence of grape.

5 Alloyed v. (过去时)合铸:Stainless steel is a type of steel alloyed with other metallic elements.

6 Circumscription n. 限界,限制:The mountains surrounding the productive agricultural land have resulted in a certain degree of environmental circumscription.

7 Amalgamation n. 组合;融合:The amalgamation of the two companies has helped to boost higher incomes.

8 Assimilating v. (进行时)吸收:The human body assimilat[es](第三人称单数现在时) the nutrients in our food by carrying out many different digestive processes.

9 Respire v. 呼吸:In some places, the air is so polluted that it seems like it is almost impossible to respire.

10 Merit n. 长处,优点:The relative merit[s](复数) of both proposals were appraised to make the final decision.

11 Offsetting v. (进行时)弥补,补偿:The cost of starting the project hardly offset[s](第三人称单数现在时) the money that can be made from it.

12 Defects n. (复数)缺陷;短处:John spotted a defect in Sally's work, and asked her to improve on it.

后记　十六岁的花季

读完赵晶颖的这本书,我的心情久久不能平静。作为她在世青中学的汉语老师,回忆和她接触的那段美好时光,是幸福的、欣慰的。那时她才12岁,她的观察能力、理解能力和对事物的感悟能力都超出了她的实际年龄。谁能想到,仅学习了两年汉语的她竟然一下就"飞"到初中7年级的语文课程中,长篇的课文,大量的生词,对于一个年仅12岁的孩子是多么大的挑战,但就凭着她那股刻苦学习的韧劲,使她在高手如林的台湾、香港学生中名列前茅。她爱写作文,更善于修改,每当我看到她的作文改到出彩的时候,兴奋之余更多的是鼓舞,鼓舞着我在教学工作中更上一层楼。如今她已经16岁了,"十六岁的花季,是一个充满理想的季节,是一个爱拼才会赢的季节"。正是因为她骨子里的那股拼劲和韧劲,才造就了她的成熟。她对事物深邃的思索,对人生深厚的理解,在这本书中充分地展示出来了。

晶颖是一个追求完美的人,每做一件事都严格地要求自己,要做到最好,她做的作品,每一份都是样板,她每次的课前演讲都能打动每一位师生,记得有一次她讲非洲儿童的故事时,尽管我曾经读过那篇文章,但经过她声情并茂的讲述,还是感动得我潸然泪下。她经常代表学校去参加各种比赛,每次比赛总是名列榜首。在德威的演唱会上她吃惊自己获得冠军的殊荣,其实在世青国际学校时,她歌唱的才华已经初露锋芒,2008年圣诞联欢会上,她载歌载舞的表演博得的满堂喝彩就已经证明了她是一个爱拼能赢的全才。

晶颖的丰富的生活经历为她提供了良好的发展空间,加之她善于观察、勤于思考,使她对每件事都有自己独特的见解,她的人生经历也因此而丰富多彩。更加难能可贵的是她时时对于思考的记载。她的《小范阿姨》就是她所写的一篇周记,当我看那篇周记时,感叹她小小年纪就有一份细腻的感情、善良的心怀。正是由于她的一点一滴的感悟,使她在学习语言的同时,不断地提高自己的人生体验。余秋雨先生曾经说:"任何一个真实的文明人,都会自觉不自觉地在心理上过着多种年龄相重叠的生活,没有这种重叠生命就会失去弹性,很容易风干和脆折。"她就是这样,将多种年龄相重叠的生活不断地回味并记录,让那一幅幅美好的景象沁入心田,滋养着全身的每个灵动的细胞,我们读来也被这多彩的而有弹性的记忆感动着。更让我感慨的是幸福美满的家庭给晶颖的健康成长奠定了坚实的基础。

多元文化的世界是绚丽的,为这样一代的学子们创造了充足的发展空间,他们从中可以开阔视野,汲取营养,开拓创新。在周围环境不断的变化中,他们会遇到不少挫折,也会增加许多的疑惑,我们从书中也读出了她的困惑,可是我们也看到了她鼓起了勇气果敢地去面对,她不断地调整视角,欣然去享受战胜困惑的过程,只有经过这段心理的历炼、精神的锤炼,才能使她学会理解、学会宽容、学会接受,才能成为真正的世界人。

愿我们的晶颖成为一名优秀的世界人。

感谢晶颖让我用我的拙笔写出我难以抑制的感情。

晶颖的朋友:何济平
2009年冬于望京